Victorien Sardou, Théodore Barrière, S. M. Quincy

A Nervous Set

Comedy in Three Acts

Victorien Sardou, Théodore Barrière, S. M. Quincy

A Nervous Set
Comedy in Three Acts

ISBN/EAN: 9783337101329

Printed in Europe, USA, Canada, Australia, Japan

Cover: Foto ©Andreas Hilbeck / pixelio.de

More available books at **www.hansebooks.com**

Comedy in Three Acts.

TRANSLATED FROM THE FRENCH OF BARRIERE AND SARDOU.

By S. M. QUINCY,

For the Boston Amateur Dramatic Club.

BOSTON :

PRINTED BY RAND, AVERY, & FRYE,

No. 3, CORNHILL.

1870.

A NERVOUS SET.

CHARACTERS.

BERGERIN, retired old bachelor.
MARTEAU, house owner.
TIBURCE, employed in post-office.
CÆSAR, nephew to Marteau.
TUFFIER, retired hardware merchant.
LOUIS, his son.
A NOTARY.
AUGUSTE, servant to Marteau.
MADAME TUFFIER.
MARION, adopted child of Marteau.
PLACIDE, housekeeper to Marteau.
LUCIE, daughter to Marteau.

The scene is laid at Batignolles, in the house owned by Marteau.

A NERVOUS SET.

ACT I.

A drawing-room. All the furniture covered with linen cases. Two side-doors in the first flats: the left, Marteau's; the right, his daughter's. The second flats oblique, forming "pan coupé." Left, door of dining-room; right, window opening on garden. The apartment is the basement. Between the two doors on the left, a piano; between the door and window on the right, a fireplace; in the back, the door of entrance; to the left of this door, a work-stand; on the right, a console, a table, and an arm-chair; on the left, a causeuse and a chair.

SCENE I.

PLACIDE, AUGUSTE, TIBURCE.

As the curtain rises, PLACIDE is in the arm-chair before the fire, reading the paper; AUGUSTE sitting on the piano-stool.

PLACIDE (*reading the paper*). We read in "The Jura Sentinel," "The first snow has just made its appearance" (*interrupting herself*). Already, — at the end of September: there's a country for you! (*turning to Auguste.*)

Well, what are you about there? How about finishing the room?

AUGUSTE. O Madame Placide! I can't tell what has come over me to-day. I feel a sort of a — kind of a — don't know what, all over. I can't get up the least energy for my work.

PLAC. Just like me: it's the weather.

AUG. (*sighing*). It's the weather.

(*Dusts the piano.* PLACIDE *reads paper;* TIBURCE, *in full dress, opens discreetly door at back, and remains an instant on the threshold.*)

TIB. (to AUG.) Monsieur Marteau, if you please. (*Silence.* AUGUSTE *dusts.* PLACIDE *reads.* TIBURCE *strikes a key on the piano, repeating, "Monsieur Marteau."*)

AUG. He's at dinner.

TIB. But still this is his reception-day?

AUG. Certainly; but even that don't prevent his dining.

TIB. That's true. (*Looks at watch.*) Twenty minutes past seven. (*Aloud*) Will he be long at dinner?

AUG. Oh! you'll have plenty of time to take a nice little walk round Batignolles. Beautiful weather! — the first day of autumn.

TIB. Thank you. I'd rather sit down.

(*Sits on chair, left.*)

PLAC. (*turns round*). Well, what is it?

AUG. Gentleman wants master.

PLAC. Suppose you take off the covers.

AUG. Yes, madame (*pulls cover of* TIBURCE's *chair*). Excuse me.

TIB. What is it?

AUG. The cover.

(TIBURCE *rises, and looks round for a seat.*)

PLAC. (to TIB.) And what may your business with master be ?

TIB. (*astonished*). Well ; pretty cool question. Moderate amount of cheek for a housekeeper.

PLAC. In the first place, I'd have you to understand I'm no housekeeper.

TIB. Oh ! excuse me (*bowing*). High official of some sort, — female beadle (*aside*).

(*Sits on chair, right of table.*)

PLAC. I am the lady in charge of M. Marteau's establishment, and have been for twenty years — do you understand ? — and I've snubbed handsomer noses than yours.

TIB. Handsomer noses.

AUG. (*pulls cover*). Excuse me.

TIB. What now ?

AUG. The cover.

TIB. (*rises provoked*). Again ?

PLAC. After all, suppose you give me the pleasure of your name ?

TIB. (*standing before fireplace*). Tiburce.

PLAC. Don't know you.

TIB. That doesn't prevent Tiburce being my name.

PLAC. And what do you do ?

TIB. Just now, I'm losing temper.

PLAC. Is that your trade ?

TIB. Yes : from nine to five, central post-office ; Mail Court ; staircase G ; Claims Bureau.

PLAC. Why, that's Monsieur Bergerin's old office before they retired him.

TIB. Well — yes, just so. My chief introduced me to Monsieur Bergerin, who presents me, this evening, to Monsieur Marteau. Does that meet your approbation ?

(*Sits on chair, at extreme right.*)

PLAC. (*aside, rising*). Goodness gracious! Now, I wonder if he is after our girls, — this chap with his white choker.

AUG. (*pulls cover as before.*) Excuse me.

TIB. (*provoked*). Again? (*Rises, and looks for seat.*)

PLAC.* Since you know Monsieur Bergerin, you might leave the parlor to us during dinner, and go up and see him.

TIB. Where does he live?

PLAC. Why, up stairs, second floor, first door. It's precious hard to find, seeing as master's house is only two stories high.

TIB. Ah! The house belongs to Monsieur Marteau?

PLAC. Who should it belong to?

TIB. And — a — Monsieur Marteau has no son?

PLAC. No. He only had a nephew, whom he has turned out of doors; but he has a young lady or two.

TIB. How do you mean " or two "?

PLAC. Why, certainly. In the first place, Mademoiselle Lucie, who is his real daughter by his deceased wife; and, secondly, Mademoiselle Marion, whom he picked up.

TIB. (*aside*). Just what they told me, — a foundling.

PLAC. Have you found out about enough now?

TIB. But I —

PLAC. Thank the Lord, you don't want for curiosity.

TIB. Excuse me. I must be allowed to remark —

PLAC.† (*holding out letters taken from table*). By the way, as you go up to M. Bergerin, just take these to —

TIB. Carry your letters! Well, by George!

PLAC. Oh, come now! I hope you'll never do any thing more dishonorable than that.

TIB. What do you say?

PLAC. All you've got to do is just to ring at Monsieur

---

* Placide, Tiburce.   † Tiburce, Placide.

Tuffier's on the first floor. You know him well enough,
—Tuffier.

Tib. Don't know him from Adam.

Plac. Oh, pshaw! Don't talk to me, — Monsieur Tuffier, master's old friend. Made his fortune in the hardware
business; an old miser and a coward — and nervous —
nervous is no word. Ah! you'd better not put him out,
nor his son Monsieur Louis either. He talks of nothing
but smashing and killing right and left; and he's a pretty
fast boy, besides, after the women. I've known him from
a baby, — he was in a manner brought up with our young
ladies, — and haven't I boxed his ears? He never bore
malice. For all that, he's going it too fast now. Now,
you ought to tell him so.

Tib. I — but since I —

Plac. You don't know him either, perhaps ?

Tib. Who ?

Plac. Monsieur Louis.

Tib. (*impatient*). Neither Pa Tuffier, Ma Tuffier, nor
young Tuffier. How they bore a fellow with their stories!
Some patience required here (*sits on causeuse*).

Aug. Excuse me.

Tib. (*furious.*) Well, what? The cover's off. What
now ?

Aug. (*holding delicately a crochet-work tidy.*) The
guipures —

Tib. Oh, d—n it! Well, I'd rather carry your letters.

Plac. Very well; only I warn you, if you want Monsieur Bergerin to turn you out, all that is needed is to loll
about over all his furniture in that style.

Tib. Oh! no sitting down there, either?

Plac. Why, it's handsomer than here, — all velvet and
silk, — and six rooms for M. Bergerin all to himself. Just
think of it, an old bachelor! It ought to make him want

to get married; but he's too selfish for that, not to mention his nerves too.

TIB. His nerves too?

PLAC. I believe you, — his too. But his aren't a circumstance compared with master's.

TIB. Monsieur Marteau?

PLAC. Yes. There's nerves for you; since he's had nothing to do. (*Violent ring in dining-room.*) There, that's his style.

TIB. (*starts*). The devil! He forewarns one anyhow. (*Another ring in the vestibule.*) Thunder!

AUG. That's M. Louis (*goes out to open*).

PLAC. (*taking cups on a waiter*). You will make his acquaintance.

TIB.* Thank you. In that style?

(*The two bells ring at once.*)

PLAC. Coming, coming. They've gone mad (*kicks open dining-room door, and enters with waiter*).

TIB. (*starts again*). By Jove, the old woman is nervous too. (*Recapitulating.*) Come, let's see : Bergerin, nervous; Pa Tuffier, nervous; young Tuffier, nervous; Pa Marteau, nervous. Why, the house is epileptic. I've made rather a lucky strike here.

LOU. (*shouts in vestibule*). Don't you trouble yourself for your visitors here, that you keep me waiting this way? Did one ever see — such rascals! (*Enters.*) Placide (*looks about*). Come, now, where has she put herself? Nobody.

TIB. (*before fireplace, aside*). Well, how about me?

LOU. (*takes no notice of TIBURCE; bangs table with cane*). Nobody. Here's a pretty household for you (*sits on arm-chair near table*). One never knows what time they dine (*looks at watch*). Now, only think, ten minutes to

---

* Placide, Tiburce.

eight. I had time enough to smoke two cigars. (*Rises, and goes to fireplace to light cigar.* TIBURCE *gets out of way quickly* LOUIS *pulls in vain: cigar won't light.*) Just my special d—d luck. I come from the Bastille — three omnibuses full —. Oh, get out! and I had to end by climbing on top; and that I do despise, for one looks so ridiculous, — just like so many calves on a market-cart.

TIB. That can't be a cigar: it's a nail he's trying to smoke.

LOU. I arrive, I ring. Wait till they come? oh, certainly! And this idiot with his nose — master's at dinner, master's got a nervous attack. Sacrebleu! I've got one myself (*catches up and flings down stool*). I should like to smash every thing here.

TIB. (*alarmed*). I'd better go up stairs, decidedly (*runs out*).

LOU. (*alone, looks after* TIBURCE). Now, who can that ass be? See him run! (*takes his hat, and reflects.*) On the whole, I'll follow his example, and be off myself. (*Exit with decided air, and slams door; then gently re-opens it, and sneaks in again.*) Yes, that's all very well; but after all, Marion, my dear little Marion, whom I can't see again to-day — and it's a week already since I squeezed her little hand (*blows kisses towards dining-room*), — O Marion! I love you and you only. You are my happiness, my joy, my gayety (*changing tone and coming down*). Yes, your gayety indeed: that's doing pretty well just now. Running about for three days; can't sleep, or eat either. I don't live, in fact. Three notes coming due, and no money; and, by George! no time to lose in getting some. So how stupid I am to be coming after this little girl, who doesn't guess I'm here, who can't even recognize my ring. That's woman all over. Coquetry, — she must be waited for. Wait now, I'll count up to a hundred: if she hasn't come by a hundred, I'm off. That'll teach you, little viper (*throws himself on causeuse back to dining-room, and counts aloud, beating time with cane*).

(MAR. *comes quietly out of dining-room, and behind him, without his hearing*).

Lou. (*counting*). Twenty-two, twenty-three, twenty-four, forty-five, fifty-seven (*stops*). It's too much : I give it up (*leans head back*). My head aches.

MAR. (*takes his hair with both hands, and pulls his head down*). That's your punishment.

Lou.* Marion.

MAR. (*holding his head*). Eight days without coming.

Lou. You are pulling my hair out. Ah!

MAR. Beg my pardon then.

Lou. I beg your pardon. Oh !

MAR. Better than that.

Lou. Pardon, pardon!

MAR. (*letting go*). Well, no : I won't pardon you. And do you know what will happen another time ? When you come, I won't speak a word (*turns her back on him, and leans on causeuse*).

Lou. Now hear me: really it isn't my fault. If you only knew.

MAR. I wish to know nothing. I don't ask your secrets.

Lou. Well, I'm in want of money — there !

MAR. Always.

Lou. Well, I should like to see how you'd manage with fifteen hundred francs salary.

MAR. Fifteen hundred francs! But what can you do with so much money ?

Lou. What do I do with it ?

---

* Louis, Marion.

Mar. Why, certainly.

Lou. Well, I commit every folly. I lead the life of a Roman satrap. Hotel, horses, carriages, and thirty-two people to dine every day, — thirty-two women.

Mar. (*piqued, comes down*). If you wouldn't make fun of me in the first place.

Lou. That's true. It's astonishing, these little girls. Because they are fed, boarded, and washed, and haven't a care but to amuse themselves.

Mar. Amuse themselves, — oh! very much. That was why I refused to go to the play last Wednesday, thinking you were coming in the evening.

Lou. You refused to go because the seats were bad; that's all.

Mar. And the ball the Wednesday before.

Lou. You refused a ball on my account? You —

Mar. Yes, sir; and a wedding-ball at that.

Lou. Oh! never in this world.

Mar. Oh! if you can —

Lou. Oh! never, never.

Mar. Well, no, there: it isn't true. I don't give up any thing for you; and I should be a fool if I did. You are too wicked and too ungrateful. Go away! What did you come for? I don't know you (*falls into arm-chair, and bursts into tears*).

Lou. You are crying.

Mar. (*hides her face*). No: on the contrary —

Lou. (*trying to remove her hands*). I tell you, you are crying.

Mar. (*turning away her head*). And I tell you no.

Lou. Marion, I am a brute, I know. My little Marion, please give me your hand. You know I can't help it. It's my nerves. Please say you are not angry with me (*kneels*).

2

Mar.* (*head averted*). Go away!

Lou. I'm not naughty. I love you dearly (*in despair*). Don't I love you? Now come.

Mar. (*feebly*). Yes. (*Lets him take her hand.*)

Lou. And you love me; now, don't you?

Mar. Why, yes.

Lou. Well, then, why do you cry? It's in my nature, you know. We can't change ourselves. But come, look at me.

Mar. (*head averted*). I don't want to: you are too wicked.

Lou. Please.

Mar. No.

Lou. I beg (*he forces her to turn her head*).

Mar. Oh, yes! that's a fine way, — if you choose to try main force. (Louis *kisses her hand : she lets him.*) Oh, well! I'm too much of a coward. If you only knew how anxious I've been, without daring to say a word either. At last, without seeming to, I managed to suggest to your mother to send the concierge to inquire at the ministry after you; and they said they'd seen you the night before. How relieved I was! But it was about time, I tell you; I was so sad and tormented.

Lou. (*holding both her hands*). Fortunately that doesn't show. You look as fresh and rosy as a —

Mar. (*piqued*). What! do you reproach me with it?

Lou. (*laughs*). I; no, indeed!

Mar. That means I ought to have fallen ill to please you, hey?

Lou. Oh, poor little darling! you ill? (*With slight raillery.*) Still you will allow, that, without falling ill exactly, you don't often lose sight of those you love for eight days without losing a little color.

* Marion, Louis.

MAR. Any way, it's better to keep it than to lose it the way you do, — gambling.

LOU. Oh! we weren't talking about me.

MAR. I ought to have lost appetite and sleep, hadn't I ?

LOU. Why, no.

MAR. I ought to have slowly pined away in tears and despair?

LOU. Not at all.

MAR. I ought to have covered myself with ashes, beat my breast, and torn out my hair, hadn't I, while you were amusing yourself?

LOU. (*goes up, impatient*). Oh! if you will talk nonsense (*sits on the arm of the chair*).

MAR. I am talking just what you think.

LOU. You are too kind.

MAR. And you are too good.

LOU. I expected this. I had much better have gone as I intended.

MAR. Oh! certainly; rather than to come resolved to pick an absurd quarrel with me.

LOU. (*jumps up*). That's my dismissal, hey ?

MAR. Just as you choose.

LOU. (*takes hat and cane*). You ought to have said so at first.

MAR.* (*bursting out*). Ah, at last! This is too much to be borne. There! you are a wicked soul, a bad heart, and an insupportable, intolerable bear. I don't love you any more. I run away, and hate you — there! (*Goes into room right, and locks door.*)

LOU. (*knocks at door*). Marion, Marion, listen to me. Marion, I'm wrong: I tell you I'm wrong — there. I'll never begin again as long as I live. Marion, I beg your pardon. My little Marion, on my knees, — I give you my

* Louis Marion.

word of honor, I'm on my knees (*kneels, and looks under door*). She's there! I see her boots (*knocks*). Open the door, Marion (*with tragedy air*). Marion, if you won't . open, I'll dash my brains out against the door. You won't open ? — well, then, — once, twice (*gets up*). Well, so much the worse. I'm a great fool after all. (*Shouts.*) You have no heart; you're a little monster: farewell! (*Undertakes to go out backwards, and comes near upsetting his father, who enters.*)

TUFFIER (*frightened*). Ah!

LOU. My father!

TUF. A chair (*falls into it, shaking all over*). Devil take you, you young scamp!

LOU. (*slapping his hands, and looking at* MARION's *door*). Oh! it isn't any thing. Come, courage!

TUF. And to-day, too, just as the weather's changing, and the wind will bring rain. My whole nervous system is in such a state. There, look at my hands (*shaking*).

LOU. Still, father, you must allow that folks shouldn't be frightened quite so easily. (*Stoops to look for* MARION's *boots.*)

TUF. (*sitting up suddenly*). Frightened! I? That's not true, you villain! I'm not timorous. I was a soldier for eighteen months, and never once afraid, I'd have you know. And I was in ten different — garrisons, — Melun, Vincennes, St. Germain —

MAD. TUF. (*enters with worsted-work in hand, and who only hears the last word of a sentence*).* Well, now, that's just another of your absurd ideas.

TUF. Well, come, then: what do you think I was talking about?

MAD. TUF. (*seated on a causeuse*). You were talking of St. Germain.

TUF. Well?

---

* Mad. Tuffier, Tuffier, Louis.

Mad. Tuf. Well, you are intending to go to see the Lacombes.

Tuf. Madame Tuffier, I have already told you a hundred times, you have the most deplorable and persistent habit —

Mad. Tuf. Goodness gracious! habit of what, then?

Tuf. Of always coming into a conversation at cross-purposes.

Mad. Tuf. I'm always at cross-purposes with you. After all, it's no hanging-matter, even for a cat. I understood, as I believed, that you had an idea of going to St. Germain; and I considered the time ill chosen, seeing that it isn't when the weather is growing cold, — when it —

Tuf. Oh! grant me patience.

Mad. Tuf. (*rising*). I had all the more right to be astonished that you should want to visit the Lacombes to-day, when they haven't been notified, because, last summer (Louis, *out of patience, tries to get his hat, unobserved*), you refused to go when they expected us (*turns, and stops* Louis) : * didn't he, Louis?

Tuf. But once more —

Mad. Tuf. (*stopping* Louis, *and continually preventing him from going out*). And, after all, these people aren't rich, — not that I despise them for that; poverty's no crime : but, any way, they don't wallow in gold, and it might incommode them terribly if we were to tumble on their backs without being expected; for, after all, when one don't expect anybody —

Tuf. (*who has tried in vain to speak, begins to rage*). Madame Tuffier!

Lou. (*getting nervous also*). Yes, mamma, pray —

Mad. Tuf. Besides it's being three miles from their house to the village —

* Louis, Mad. Tuffier, Tuffier.

2*

Tuf. Madame Tuffier!

Lou. (*aside*). Oh! isn't mamma exasperating?

Mad. Tuf. And all to get a wretched mutton-chop —

Lou. and Tuf. (*shout*). Enough, enough!

(Tuffier *is taken with another attack, and falls into chair near table.*)

Mad. Tuf. (*to* Lou.) Oh, very well, very well!

(*Sits down to her work,* r.)

Enter Bergerin and Tiburce.

Bergerin (*followed by* Tiburce). What's the matter?

Tuf. (*groans*). She will kill me, Bergerin.

Mad. Tuf. (*rises*). All that just because —

Tuf. (*screams*). Are you going to begin again? Oh, my nerves, my nerves!

(*Madame* Tuffier *shrugs shoulders, and sits.*)

Lou. (*loosening his father's cravat*). I say, if you should help me a little, Monsieur Bergerin.

Berg. (*turning his back on* Tuffier, *and coming down,* l.)* O my boy! you mustn't count on me for these affairs, if I know myself — the mere sight of a suffering animal — I couldn't look at Tuffier now for the world.

Tuf. (*coming to*). Ah!

Lou. (*shakes him*). There, there! courage!

Berg. Stop! the mere thought that my poor friend is there nearly fainting — I am forced to sit down (*sits on causeuse, turning his back on* Tuffier).

Tiburce (*looking at him*). Now, that is astonishing. To look at you, one would never think you so susceptible.

Berg. (*seated, and reclining*). I, — why, I'm nothing but a bundle of nerves, young man. Why, the least emotion, any thing contrary, a change of weather — Now

---

* Tiburce, Bergerin, Tuffier, Mad. Tuffier.

to-day, for instance, this change of wind, bringing dry
weather —

TUF. (*sitting up*). Bringing rain (*to* LOUIS *and his
wife*). Why don't you tell him it's going to bring rain ?

BERG. (*to* TIB.). So you can imagine what strict ré-
gime I have to follow, — a calm, well-ordered life ; regular
promenade ; good cuisine ; theatre very often (plays that
make you laugh) ; warm rooms ; good carpets ; constant
care to avoid all painful impressions, all sights of suffering
or poverty. Oh, I can't abide the sight of poverty !

LOU. (*aside*). This man will give me an attack of
nerves. I shall just leave. (*Exit suddenly.*)

BERG. (*continuing*). I can't marry, because a woman,
quarrels, jealousy, love itself, — they are all things that
affect one too much. One must, — and then one isn't al-·
ways, — and then — the woman — you understand, and
the children. Ah ! the children especially. A child cries ;
he suffers ; he's teething : you must get up — at night —
run for the doctor — and see my child in pain — poor little
dear ! I know myself. I should go right into the country.

MAD. TUF. (*at mantelpiece, where she has gone for her
scissors ; hears the last word*). Ah ! you've bought it,
then ?

TUF. What ?

MAD. TUF. Why, that house in the country you were
talking about, isn't it, — somewhere near Colombes ?

TUF. We are not talking of that.

BERG. No, madame ; I was saying —

MAD. TUF. (*crosses to* BERG.) So much the better. I
confess I was astonished that you should have intended to
settle for good in the country : it is so monotonous.*

TUF. (*in despair*). Now she'll never stop.

---

* Tiburce, Bergerin, Ma l. Tuffier, Tuffler.

MAD. TUF. You know, too, they offered Monsieur Tuffier a receiver-generalship at Pithiviers.

TUF. Bergerin, what time is it?

MAD. TUF. But I insisted on his refusing it.

TUF. Well, I did refuse it.

MAD. TUF. And you did well.

TUF. Well, that's settled.

MAD. TUF. Yes, sir, you did well; for I should have died there.

BERG. (*aside, rising*). By George! in that case —

MAD. TUF. (*to* BERG.) Only think of that, sir!

BERG. (*tranquilly*). I am thinking of it, madam.

MAD. TUF. Leave Batignolles at my age?

BERG. Yes.

TUF. Oh!

MAD. TUF. For I was born at Batignolles, sir, in Long Monk Street.

BERG. There's no harm in that.

MAD. TUF. My father was an apothecary.

BERG. Well, we're none of us perfect. (*Sits.*)

TUF. (*who hasn't got in a word*). But don't answer her, Bergerin.

MAD. TUF. (*sentimentally*). You men don't care for the native soil that saw your birth; but we, — we hold to it.

TUF. But who's going to take away your soil?

MAD. TUF. Goodness knows I've often tried to reason myself out of it: I've said to myself, that one's country should be anywhere with the beloved object; (*aside to* BERGERIN) but then, in the first place, my husband never was the beloved object.

BERG. That simplifies the question, — greatly.

MAD. TUF. Besides, why should he insist upon my burying myself alive in the provinces?

BERG. (*to* TUF.) Yes, why, indeed? — why?

TUF. (*to his wife*). Why, can't you see that Bergerin is just chaffing you?

BERG. Well! — I like that.

MAD. TUF. That's a lie.

TIB. (*aside*). This doesn't seem to be a family of turtle-doves.

MAD. TUF. You judge other people by yourself.

BERG. (*seeking to calm her*). Madame!

MAD. TUF. No, sir: that man is never happy unless he can insult me, — and all that because he married me without a fortune.

TUF. (*screams*). Here comes something else.

MAD. TUF. (*crosses,* R.) But you were old, and I was young, and should be still, if it wasn't for all the suffering you have caused me.

TUF. Oh!

MAD. TUF. (*crying*). Some day, — do you understand, sir? — I shall go home to my mother.

TUF. (*screams*). Enough, enough!

TIB. (*aside*). One must fall ill very easily in this house.

Enter PLACIDE.

PLAC. (*enters precipitately from dining-room*). Hold your tongues!

ALL. What is it?

PLAC. Monsieur Marteau — he's got his nervous attack.

TIB. The devil! (*To* BERGERIN.) I say, then, don't present me just now.

BERG. Bah! he's always just so.

MAD. TUF.* I'm going home.

---

* Tiburce, Bergerin, Placide, Mad. Tuffier. Tuffler.

BERG. You leave us?

TUF. Of course. Madame Tuffier might possibly be useful now, if Marteau is sick : so she goes off as she came, — mal apropos.

MAD. TUF. Monsieur Tuffier, you are a mere insect, a reptile. (*Exit.*)

PLAC. Here he comes: there's a face for you! By jingo, I'm off! (*Exit.*)

.(MARTEAU *enters from dining-room, hands behind his back, head hanging mournfully. All regard him in silence. He shakes* TUFFIER'S *hand without looking at him, and passes without a word. The same with* BERGE-RIN. *Coming to* TIBURCE, *who tries to avoid him, he takes his hand without looking at him ; is about to shake it ; raises his head, and regards* TIBURCE *with amazement ; drops his hand, turns his back upon him, and crosses from left to right to take chair near the table.*)

BERG. (*to* MART.) You are not well, eh ?
MART. No.
BERG. Nerves?
MART. Yes.
TUF. Change of wind ?
MART. Yes.
BERG. I said so. Dry weather.
TUF. ʃ Rain.
MART. Yes, a storm.
BERG. (*to* MART.) Supposing you tried Pulverma-cher's chains. (MARTEAU *opens newspaper.*)
TUF. Or Paullinia. (*To* MARTEAU, *who holds out paper to him.*) Do you want me to read ? (MARTEAU *makes affirmative sign, indicates the passage, and sits on the causeuse.*)
TUF. (*reads*). Ten thousand francs reward to the man

who can cure an inveterate nervous affection. Apply at Monsieur M's, 35 Church Street, Batignolles. (*Spoken.*) You? (*Affirmative sign from* MARTEAU.) And somebody has come? (MARTEAU *raises ten fingers.*)

BERG. Quacks? (*Affirmative sign.*)

TUF. Well, where are they? (MARTEAU *extends foot.*) Kicked out? (*Affirmative sign.*)

TIB. (*half aloud*). Well, that gives him a chance to vent his nerves on somebody (*makes the same gesture of kicking*).

MART. (*rises, stares at him with surprise, and pulls* BERGERIN'S *sleeve, indicating* TIBURCE). Where does that creature come from?

BERG. (*to* TIB.) Ah! now you're caught: so I'll present you. My dear Marteau, this is Monsieur Tiburce, employed in my old bureau in the post-office.

TIB. (*bows to* MART.*) Mail Court, Staircase G, Claim Bureau.

MART. Well, what do you claim?

TIB. (*taken aback*). Why, good heavens!—I—

MART. As for me, I claim nothing: so it must be you.

TIB. Well—that is—I—(*to* BERGERIN), can't you help me?

BERG. (*seated on causeuse*). Oh, no! my dear friend, I can't: that might bring on a discussion; and that, if I know myself, would be just fatal.

MART. Well, sir. Come, speak up.

BERG. (*nudging him*). Speak up.

TIB. Well, the fact is—

BERG. Come, go ahead.

TIB. (*bowing to* MART). Dear and honored sir—ahem. An official of the Central Post-office, Mail Court, Staircase G—

* Bergerin, Tiburce, Marteau, Tuffier.

BERG.   Yes, that's agreed to.

TIB.   After serving a year as — a — supernumerary, and at present salaried at the rate ‚of twelve hundred francs per annum, to which must be added an income of twelve thousand francs left me by my deceased parents; being certain, besides, of rapid promotion, thanks to the protection of my chief and of his eminent predecessor (*bowing to* BERGERIN).

BERG.   Hear, hear!

TIB.   I venture (*bows to* MARTEAU), sir, to solicit the unequalled honor of your alliance, and aspire to the hand of your fair daughter.

MART.   Lucie?

TIB.   No: the other, if you please.

MART.   Marion?

TIB.   Mademoiselle Marion.   Yes, sir.

MART.   Do you know Marion?

TIB.   From having had the honor of dancing with her quite often this winter.

MART.   (*to the rest*).   Now, tell me, isn't this just of a piece with my pursuing fate?   My dinner went wrong, the mutton wasn't cooked, the chicken was burnt, the coffee was cold, my digestion was out of order; and all that was wanting to upset it entirely was just such an idiotic performance as this, and, of course, here it is brought on. Oh! it's my destiny.   It's some trick you want to play me, — come, isn't it? *   (*To* BERGERIN.)

BERG.   (*takes snuff*).   I, — I scout the idea: decide just as you choose.

MART.   How can I decide any thing?   Do I know the gentleman? have I ever danced with him?   (*Walks up and down.*)

TIB.   (*humbly*).   I must confess I have not had that honor.

* Bergerin (seated), Marteau, Tiburce, Tuffier.

MART. Do I know his good and bad points? — his temperament above all; for that's the most vital question, — a son-in-law's temperament. Now, is his a nervous temperament?

TIB. No, sir.

MART. (*continuing his walk, and going up*). Sanguine?

TIB. No.

MART. (*coming down*). Bilious?

TIB. No.

MART. Bilioso-sanguine?

TIB. Not at all.

MART. Nervoso-sanguine?

TIB. Not that, either.

MART. Nervoso-bilioso-sanguine?

TIB. (*frightened*). Devil a bit!

MART. (*stops short, to* BERG.) I say — he's got no temperament at all.

BERG. Well, how should I know?

TIB. But —

MART. No temperament, therefore no character; *ergo*, he isn't a man. (*Goes up and pokes fire.*)

TIB. (*indignant*). What! On the contrary —

TUF. (*to* TIB.) Well, well, we'll see. Really, now, what is your temperament?

TIB. But, sacrebleu! no one ever asked me in my life.

BERG. Why don't you answer?

TIB. (*half aloud*).* At this rate, it seems that I must absolutely have a temperament of some sort.

TUF. (*to* BERG.) Of course.

TIB. Well, let's see. (*To* BERGERIN.) Help me a little, can't you; you're there. Couldn't I be sanguine, for instance?

---

* Bergerin, Tiburce, Tuffler, Marteau.

3

MART. (*turns round, tongs in hand*). Sanguine, *ergo* predisposed to apoplexy and congestion. Danger for the wife, for the children, for the father-in-law. Candidate rejected.

TIB. No, no! I was saying I wasn't sanguine at all, but bilious. Will that suit you, — bilious?

MART. Bilious, *ergo* predisposed to melancholy, blue devils, and insanity. Candidate rejected.

TIB. Excuse me, I recollect now. I am not bilious, — far from it.

MART. (*quickly coming down*). Then you're nervous? *

TIB. Nervous?

MART., BERG., *and* TUF. Yes?

TIB. (*embarrassed*). Why, in fact I am, — and then I'm not.

ALL THREE. Explain yourself.

TIB. Well, it's just here. I am if you wish it; but, if you don't wish it —

MART. You had better believe I don't wish it. It would only need a nervous son-in-law to drive me mad.

ALL THREE. Yes, indeed.

MART. Examine yourself, therefore, young man, and let's be quick. If you are not of a sweet and obliging disposition, and easy to live with; if you are not apt in choosing topics of conversation agreeable to me; if you can't ring the bell, laugh, and blow your nose, without noise, talk on a low key, and never stir except in case of absolute necessity —

TIB. But I —

MART. In short, if you continue to use the hair-oil you've got on now, and if all your waistcoats are of that loud and insulting style, you're not my man. Candidate rejected.

TIB. Well, I —

* Bergerin, Tiburce, Marteau, Tuffier.

Mart. And, to convince you that I'm in earnest, you may know that I've just turned out of doors a young fellow of wit and education, my sister's own son, my nephew Cæsar, just because he aggravated my nerves. So examine yourself, and if you are of a nature to get provoked, and to provoke me, and to get us both exhausted (*goes to sit on chair near table*) —

Tib. (*following*). But allow me —

Mart. You understand, I hope, that I've no desire to get rid of Marion ?

Tib. Most assuredly, I —

Mart. And that, when I want to marry her off —

Tib. Oh! I don't doubt —

Mart. I shall have no trouble in finding —

Tib. Most indubitably —

Mart. (*for some time impatient ; jumps up, and bursts out*). D—n it, man, let me speak ! don't catch up every word that way.

Tib. Yes, sir. (*Aside.*) What a fire-cracker for a pa-in-law !

Mart. I was saying, then, that I should have no trouble in finding a son-in-law at least equally good-looking and talented.

Tib. (*vexed*). But —

Mart. For I imagine you'd hardly set the river on fire.

Tib. (*to* Berg.) How d—d aggravating he is !

Mart. (*signing him to approach*). You're not handsome, either ; (*movement of* Tiburce*, who crosses,* R.) but that I don't require. The vital question for me, as I said before, is the temperament of my son-in-law. I don't intend that my poor Marion shall have to suffer from her husband's nerves, like my departed angel ; for I'd be willing to bet that it was my nerves that killed Madame Marteau.

BERG. (*tranquilly*).. I'm firmly convinced of it.

MART. So I've just sworn that my two daughters shall marry no matter who and no matter what, so long as no matter what's not nervous. There you are now, nailed!

TIB. Why, my dear sir, I'm just your man exactly; for I'm not in the least nervous. I'll take my Bible oath I'm not nervous.

MART. Oh! you'll swear it, I don't doubt; it's very easy to swear. (*Aside.*) We'll try that in half a minute (*gives* TIBURCE, *when he least expects it, violent slap on shoulder with loud yell; then catches his wrist with one hand, and pulls out watch with the other*).

TIB. Thunder! You've most dislocated my shoulder.

MART. (*counting pulse*). That's nothing. (*Aside.*) Good pulse, steady and calm. Now for another test (*goes to sofa*). Come here, young man (*makes the motion of scratching the velvet the wrong way*); just try that a little in order to see —

TIB. Scratch the velvet! (*Aside.*) Here's an examination! (*Scratches away furiously.*)

BERG. *and* TUF. (*agacés*). Enough, enough!

MART. (*teeth on edge*). Very well, young man.

TIB. Is it over?

MART.* Not yet. (*Offers knife and cork taken from sideboard.*) Take this knife, now, and this cork, and cut. (TIBURCE *cuts; the cork squeaks.* TUFFIER, BERGERIN, *and* MARTEAU *grit their teeth.*)

MART., TUF., *and* BERG. (*shout*). Enough, enough!

TIB. There! (TUFFIER *snatches away knife and cork.*)

MART. (*with admiration*). Didn't flinch, didn't grit his teeth, didn't wink. Admirable!

* Tiburce, Bergerin (higher up), Marteau, Tuffier.

Berg. Astounding ! *

Mart. (*solemnly*). That will suffice, young man : you are not nervous. I hereby extend you my permission to aspire to the hand of Marion.

Tib. What happiness !

Mart. Why, you feel nothing: you are a real machine. Lord bless my soul, you are just the man I've been wanting. Now I can be just as nervous as I d—n please, and always have somebody to fall back on.

Tuf. (*squeezing* Tib.'s *hand*). And so can I.

Berg. (*ditto*). And so can I.

Tib.† Ah ! but excuse me.

Mart. Son-in-law without nerves, come to my arms (*embrace*).

Enter, Louis.

Lou. (*enters in time to hear* Marteau. *Screams*). Son-in-law !

Berg., Tuf., *and* Mart. (*start*). Ah !

Mart. Ah ! d—n that fellow.

Lou. ‡ This gentleman your son-in-law ?

Mart. Undoubtedly.

Lou. (*shouts*). No: that shall never be.

Mart. Eh ?

Tuf. Will you hold your tongue ?

Lou. I won't have him marry Marion : I forbid him to marry her.

Tib. (*amazed*). I say, though —

Mart. Leave the room, sir !

Lou. Yes, I forbid him ; and, if he does marry her, I'll kill him.

---

* Tuffier, Tiburce, Marteau, Bergerin.
† Tuffier, Tiburce, Marteau (behind him), Bergerin.
‡ Tiburce, Tuffier, Louis, Marteau, Bergerin.

3*

ALL. Good God !

TIB. (*frightened*). Sir !

LOU. (*stamps and strikes chair*). Yes, I'll kill him.

TUF. He'll kill him !

MART. He's killing him !

BERG. He's killed him !

LOU. (*beside himself*). And I'll set the house afire.

MART. My house afire !

TIB., TUF., *and* BERG. (*losing their heads*). Fire, fire !

Enter, CÆSAR.

CÆSAR (*bursts in*). Fire ? Where ?

LOU. (*runs to* CÆSAR). Ah, Cæsar !

MART. (*in centre, extended on arm-chair, and unable to stir*). My nephew.

CÆS. (*to* LOU.) Whereabouts ? where is it ?

LOU. What ?

CÆS. The fire.

LOU. Oh ! nowhere.

TUF. (*leaning back,* L.) Oh, my nerves !

BERG. (*ditto,* R.) My nerves !

MART. (*centre*). My nerves !

TIB. (*aside*). Murder ! What sort of a house is this ?

CÆS. Then we're not afire here ? All right. (*Bows to* MARTEAU.) Good-morning, uncle ! I'm pretty well, I thank you : how are you ?

MART. (*still reclining, and in plaintive voice*). Wretch, I thought I had turned you out with my malediction !

CÆS. You're right, uncle, you did. But you see I had to bring it back. Nobody would lend me a cent on it.

MART. (*sits up*). You don't say ! Well, you rascal ! now I intend that you shall clear out. Who asked you to come inside my doors again ?

CÆS. (*tranquilly*). Why, you did.

MART. I ?

CÆS. (*takes out paper*). Just read there : " Ten thousand francs reward to the man who can cure " —

MART. My advertisement!

CÆS. (*folding paper*). Ten thousand francs, — that's just about my figure; and when I saw, " 35 Church Street, Batignolles," I said to myself, " By Jove! it's Uncle Marteau; and we can keep it snug in the family; come along." And it seems I've arrived just in time, eh ?

MART. (*rises*). Listen to me.

CÆS. Yes.

MART. Do you want to cure me really ?

CÆS. Really.

MART. Then be off at once.

CÆS. No, no, no! I don't treat my patients that way. I should be no sooner gone than you'd be off in another (*imitates nervous fit*) — I must make a perfect cure, — one that folks will talk about.

MART. (*to* BERG.) Suppose I call the watch ?

CÆS. Watch! Oh! you won't need a watcher: I'll take care of that. (MARTEAU, *in despair, raises his hands to heaven.*) (CÆSAR *turns to* TUFFIER *and* BERGERIN). But don't interrupt your affairs, I beg of you : that don't affect the treatment. What were you talking about so lively when I came in ?

TUF. We were talking of marriage.

CÆS. (*behind table*). Marriage! Do you always discuss it in that style? Who's going to be married, — you ?

MART. (*starts*). I ?*

CÆS. No? Then it must be Monsieur Bergerin going to marry Placide.

BERG. Well, that's flattering. (*Goes up near window.*)

* Tiburce, (Louis and Tuffier higher up), Marteau, Cæsar, Bergerin.

Cæs. (*points to* Lou.)   Then it's the young one and
Lucie.

Lou.   No, indeed !

Cæs.   So much the better.   Then it's to Marion ?

Mart.   Likely story !

Cæs. (*comes down before fireplace*, R.*)   Well, what
is there so very astonishing in that ?   I know little Louis,
— I know him from a child : he is a little crazy, but —

Mart.   A little !   He needs a strait-waistcoat, that's all.

Lou. (*between his father and* Mart.)   O Monsieur
Marteau !

Tuf. (*piqued, rising*).   But, any way, I don't see
that you are called upon to put yourself out in the matter.
I believe we have not yet asked you for your daughter.

Cæs. (*to* Tuf.)   No ; but that's what you ought to do.

Lou.   Of course it is.

Mart.   Is it ?   Well, you'd better try it.

Tuf.   Thank you ; I guess not.

Mart.   Why, he isn't a man : he's a Voltaic pile, a
Leyden jar, an electric battery.

Lou.   But Monsieur Marteau, after all —

Tuf.   Will you go away, you wicked boy ?

Lou.   Oh ! that's the style, is it ?   (*Knocks hat down
on his head.*)   Well, no ; I won't go away.

Mart.   Do you see ?   The rascal !

Cæs.   Come, come.   He's a fine fellow, and so am I ; and
you — you're one of the best men in the world, with all
your oddities ; and I hope you don't entertain the absurd
idea of giving Marion that gentleman with his funny head
for a husband.   (*Points at* Tiburce.)

Tib.   Sir !

Mart.   Precisely so, sir.   I do entertain that grotesque
idea ; and I was only waiting for your consent.

* Tiburce, Louis, Tuffier, Marteau, Bergerin near window, Cæsar.

C.ᴇs. All right. I refuse it.

Mᴀʀᴛ. Did you ever!

(Bᴇʀɢᴇʀɪɴ *comes down, and sits on chair at table to read paper.*)

C.ᴇs. Bad marriages! Why, one sees nothing else; all the more reason to make a good one once in a while.: so that's arranged. Bergerin shall marry Placide; Louis, Marion; and I, Lucie. What do you say to that idea?

Mᴀʀᴛ. (*stupefied*). I say (*to* Bᴇʀɢᴇʀɪɴ *and* Tᴜғғɪᴇʀ) by George! he is superb.

C.ᴇs. In the first place, I'm superb (that's one advantage); and then I love the dear child (that's an idea of mine, and a pretty old one) : she knows it; and she don't say no: so she means yes; and there it is, then — settled.

Mᴀʀᴛ. (*to* Bᴇʀɢ. *and* Tᴜғ.) I declare, I don't know if I'm dreaming. What! here's a rascal whom I've turned out, who comes back as brassy as you please, and marries off Peter, and marries off Paul. No: but just look at it now; isn't it too good a joke? Oh! you'll lay down the law in my house, will you? Well, now, perhaps this marriage wouldn't have come off; for after all, on reflection, this fellow didn't suit me exactly.

Tɪʙ. Eh!

Mᴀʀᴛ. But he shall marry her now, I'm determined, if it's only to make you burst with rage.

C.ᴇs. So you will marry your daughter out of spite.

Mᴀʀᴛ. Out of spite if you choose; but I'll marry her. You'll see then if I'm the master in my own house. And as to your fine projects in regard to Lucie (*strikes* Tᴜғғɪᴇʀ *on shoulder*) — now see how I'll humiliate him, if I don't bring him down a peg or two (*strikes* Bᴇʀɢᴇʀɪɴ *on shoulder, who wakes up, and goes to sit on chair behind table*).

Cæs. Ah! now: suppose we see what he's going to do.* (*Sits*, R.)

Mart. Worthless rascal! do you talk of being married?

Cæs. Why, yes.

Mart. Have you got even an occupation, a trade? What do you call yourself?

Cæs. A philosopher, uncle.

Mart. Where do you carry on that business?

Cæs. In the open air.

Mart. And you live by it?

Cæs. Oh, no!

Berg. Then, how does he live?

Mart. Yes, how do you live?

Cæs. I don't live, uncle. I just exist; and even that's something.

Mart. Anyway, you eat well?

Cæs. No, I don't: I eat ill.

Mart. What did I tell you? — a mere Bohemian.

Berg. *and* Tuf. A Bohemian!

Cæs. Give me your income, and I'll settle down.

Mart. Earn it then, lazy.

Cæs. Ah! now the murder's out, — lazy. Well, now, I advise you to call me lazy: it sounds well, — you who only had the trouble of inheriting your wife's money, and who never did in your whole life one-quarter of the work I do every day in order to pay my rent. (*Striking on the books, which* Bergerin *prudently takes away one by one.*) Have you ever been as I have, one after the other, tutor, — work fit for a dog; bailiff's clerk, cashiered for his humanity; employé, ridiculed for his zeal; writer, unpopular because original; salesman, book-keeper, printer, trans-

* Tiburce, Louis, Tuffler, Marteau, Bergerin, Cæsar.

lator, inventor, cheated for the benefit of others, taken advantage of, lived on, and always just missing a million for the want of a hundred thousand, a hundred thousand for the want of ten thousand, ten thousand for the want of five hundred, and five hundred for the want of five francs? (*Final blow on table, which* BERGERIN *draws away.*)

MART. (*agacé*). Great Heavens!

CÆS.* Ah! you call me lazy, — you whose only work is to scold your servants, and to pet your imaginary and pretended nerves.

TUF. *and* BERG. Our pretended nerves!

MART. (*clinching his fists*). Brouhouhou!

CÆS. Yes, Brouhouhou. Stick your head in a bucket of water: that'll calm you. What are these make-believe men made of? — fastidious as cats.

MART., TUF., BERG. Cats!

CÆS. Yes, cats, — just such nervous and lazy animals as you, and very nearly as selfish. Monsieur Bergerin rolls himself up in his eider-down, and won't think about those who are freezing, — a cat! Monsieur Tuffier has a nervous attack. Good God! you mustn't ask him for money; he'd have a fit, — a fit of avarice and selfishness, — a cat! Monsieur Marteau has *his* nerves: that means Monsieur Marteau has nothing to do, and so he must yawn, get bored, and occupy himself in driving other people mad. Tom-cats, tom-cats, tom-cats! †

MART. Grant me patience! Once, twice, and three times — will you be off?

CÆS. No! I came to cure you; and, by all the devils, I will cure you.

MART. Whether I will or not?

* Tiburce, Tuffier, Cæsar, Bergerin, Marteau.
† Tiburce, Tuffier, Cæsar, Marteau, Bergerin.

Cæs. Whether you will or not, and Bergerin too, and Tuffier also, in spite of them, and all the house too, — in ten visits at a thousand francs each.

Mart. Well, just have the front to present yourself here once more —

Cæs. Oh! I shall have it.

Mart. I'll lock the door.

Cæs. I'll get in at the window.

Mart. (*furious, held by* Tuf.) My cane!

Cæs. There's for you! And we shall all enjoy a pure and unmixed felicity — he with Marion —

Lou. Yes, yes!

Cæs. (*taking his hat*). And I with Lucie. Such being the case, I think that will do for the first day of treatment. (*To* Tiburce.) Come on, young man ; say good-by to the company, and come along with me.

Tib. I?

Cæs. Come along : you'd get spoiled here.

Tib. Here! let go.

Cæs. (*pulling him along*). First prescription, uncle : see you again to-morrow.

Berg., Mart., Tuf. Oh!

Cæs. Sta-boy! cats, cats! (*Runs out, dragging* Tiburce. Marteau *falls exhausted on chair.*)

End of Act I.

ACT II.

THE SAME SCENE.

Lucie *playing scales on piano ;* Marion, R., *winding clock on mantelpiece ;* Marteau, *centre, seated in large arm-chair, feet on stool, is enveloped with electric chains, which prevent his moving.* Clock *strikes, successively, nine, half-past, ten, half-past, &c.* Placide, *at back, dusting in ante-chamber.*

Mart. (*after pause, angrily*). Marion!

Marion. Papa? (*Continues to turn hands.*)

Mart. (*gently*). No, I mustn't get angry. With these electro-magnetic chains on, the currents, and then the fluid,—no one can tell what mightn't happen. (*Very gently.*) Haven't you most done, my darling?

Mar. But, papa, I must set it right.

Mart. Supposing you should skip some, my pet?

Mar.· What an idea, pa! It would strike all wrong. I'll be done in a minute. There's only eleven and twelve : it's half-past twelve now. (*Clock strikes eleven.*)

Mart. (*aside*). Now, some clocks would arrange it so as to have only one or two hours to strike; but that fellow—I believe he just does it on purpose—stops so as to have to be swung round the entire circle.

Mar. (*striking the half-hour*). Courage, papa! only twelve left.

Mart. It's astonishing, now, what these small articles can invent in the way of aggravation. Now, when I try to wind that fellow up, I'm sure to find a hand over one

4

of the holes : he knows it aggravates me, and never fails
to do it. (*Clock strikes twelve.*)   The devil and Tom
Walker ! it's enough to drive one mad !   Lucie !

Luc. (*without stopping her scales*).   Papa ?

Mart. (*aside*).   But I forgot I mustn't get angry.
(*Gently.*)   Lucie, my love, is it absolutely necessary that
you should do that ?

Luc.   Play my scales ?

Mart.   Yes.

Luc.   Why, papa, I must learn.

Mart.   That's true : she must learn.   I'll have that
piano carried into the garden.

Luc.   That'll keep it in good tune.

Mar.   Yes, indeed.

Mart.   *A propos* of gardens, just call Placide, now I
think of it.

　　　(Marion *goes to door at back to call* Placide.)

Luc. (*leaving piano*).   Why, papa !   what's all that
you've got coiled round you ?

Mart. (*frightened*).   Don't touch !

Luc.   Will he bite ?

　　　(Marion *and* Placide *come down.*)

Mart.   It's electric.

All Three.   Electric !

Mart.   Like lightning.   In fact, the lightning holds
me in its mighty arms, so I daren't stir.   The least spark —

Plac.*   Well, that's an idea, — to wind that round your
body to keep the thunder off.

Mart.   You ignoramus !   It's to restore the nervous
circulation : it's electricity.

Plac.   Electricity !   well, I know that as well as you.
It's a telegraph, hey, that the little post-office chap

---

* Lucie, Marion, Marteau, Placide.

brought you? for that's the way they send their letters now; and three-quarters get lost on the road.

MART. Ah, good heavens! have you done? If so, will you do me the favor to listen to me?

PLAC. Well, what is it now?

MART. It's this; that, if my nephew Cæsar presents himself —

PLAC. Well, I'll let him in. What then?

MART. You'll shut the door in his face. Do you understand?

PLAC. I think I see myself. Why should I go shutting doors in this young man's face, who has always been so polite to me?

MART. Because he isn't to me.

PLAC. Oh! I don't intend to be mixed up in your foolishness. Settle your quarrel your own way: it's none of my business.

MART. By heavens!

PLAC. (*without listening to him*). No, no, no, no!

MART. Oh! you're lucky that the lightning's got me now, and that I daren't get in a passion.

PLAC. Oh! Well, of course nobody must say such a thing; but if that could curb your temper a little, and prevent your being so outrageous —

MART. Lucie! Marion!

LUC. *and* MAR. Papa!

MART. Turn her out. I feel I'm going off.

LUC. Yes, papa.

MAR. (*to* PLAC.) Get away.

PLAC. (*tranquilly*). It's only the telegraph working. Listen!

MART. (*rises furious*). I dismiss you!

PLAC. (*laughs*). Yes, sir.

MART. But not like the other times, you understand: now it's for good.

PLAC. (*laughs*).   Yes, sir.   Well, if that's the way it calms his nerves —

MART. (*breaks chain, and throws it at her*).   There!

PLAC.   Mercy!   (*Runs out laughing.*)

MAR. *and* LUC. (*seek to restrain him*).   Papa, dear!

MART.   Take that too.   (*Throws another piece after her in the vestibule; comes back, and falls into chair.*) She'll kill me!

LUC. (*seeking to calm him*).   There, there, papa!

MAR.   How can one get into such a state?

MART.   I'm not in such a state.   You're a pair of little fools!   Go to your piano, and play your scales.

LUC. *and* MAR.   Yes, papa.   (*Both sit at piano.*)

MART.   Only to think that I've been in chains since seven this morning, to arrive at this result!   (LUCIE *and* MARION *begin to play scales for four hands.*)   And now it's one, and I'm not even shaved, and that young man will be here.   O Marion!

MAR. (*playing*).   Papa?

MART.   I order you to give a good reception to Mon sieur Tiburce, who will be here directly.   Do you hear me?

MAR. (*playing*).   Yes, papa.

MART.   And if you ever dare to listen to that villain of a Louis!   The scoundrel has told you he loves you, has he?

MAR. (*playing*).   Yes, papa.

MART.   Yes, papa! — did you ever?   And the other chap, who graciously lends his countenance to his cousin's offers of marriage — ah!   I'll give you cousins enough. (*Knocking on ceiling from story above.*)   I'm talking to you, Ma'amselle Lucie.   Do you hear?

LUC. (*playing*).   Yes, papa.

MART.   I forbid you — (*Knocking on ceiling.*)   Who's that up there pounding?

Luc. (*playing*). Yes, papa.

Mart. Well, I forbid you — (*Knocking redoubled.*) But who the devil is that pounding up there?

Luc. *and* Mar. (*playing*). Yes, papa.

Mart. (*exasperated*). Oh, yes, papa! With that piano, and bang, bang, bang, I don't know where I've got to. Ah! if the day begins this way — (*Bursts out.*) Are you going to stop?

(*Enter* Bergerin *with tongs, and* Tuffier *with cane.*)

Tuf. Why, good God! make them stop.

Berg. Are you going to stop?

Mart.* Was it you, then, pounding over my head?

Tuf. (*points to* Berg.) He was pounding over mine.

Mart. That's very witty: it's an excellent joke for men of our age.

Tuf. What do you mean by a joke?

Berg. Well, that's a good one. Here have I been hearing for half an hour (*imitates scales*) — you'd say it was a dance going on. I thought it was Madame Tuffier, and so I knocked at Tuffier.

Tuf. And I was knocking back at Bergerin.

Mart.† And that's the way you expect to prevent their playing the piano!

Berg. Let 'em play, my dear friend, let 'em play; only one at a time, file firing, — one down, and another come on, — not volley by platoons.

Tuf. Only they don't play tunes (*imitates scale*).

Mar. Well, how about pieces for two?

Luc. The four-handed pieces.

Tuf. There aren't any four-handed pieces.

Berg. Nature has foreseen the case, and only given us two hands.

---

* Bergerin, Marion, Lucie higher up, Tuffier, Marteau.

† Bergerin, Marion, Marteau, Lucie, Tuffier.

4*

Tuf. (*knocks with cane*).   And when we use them well —

Mart.   Oh! I heard you.

Berg.   Well, if we had both pounded together —

Tuf.   A four-handed piece.

Berg.   Here's about the effect it would have had. (*Both knock with all their might.*)

Mart.   Here, would you like to know my opinion? Well, I pity you, I pity you.

Mar.   There! Now we sha'n't be able to play any more: that's pleasant.

Tuf.   Very pleasant for us.

Enter Madame Tuffier.

Mad. Tuf.   Why do you pay any attention to them: aren't they always complaining about something? (*Sits behind table.   Marteau sits on causeuse.*)

Tuf.*   Ah! you've come into the conversation for a wonder.

Mad. Tuf.   Well, who's a better right?   I say it's all affectation.

Tuf.   Like the perfumes, which you can't smell without going off in hysterics.

Mad. Tuf.   It isn't the same thing.

Tuf.   It is the same thing.

Mad. Tuf., Luc., Mar.   It isn't the same thing.

Berg. (*aside*).   There! three women on you.   Get out of that!

Mar.   Perfumes enervate you at once.

Luc.   Go into your head.

Mar.   Especially pomade: like that gentleman's yes-

---

* Bergerin (standing), Marteau (seated), Marion, Mad. Tuffier, and Lucie (seated), Tuffier (standing).

terday (*to her father*), — Monsieur Tiburce, whom I've
danced with this season. Heavens! didn't he smell of
vanilla. Whew!

ALL THREE. Whew!

MART. That's true; but he has promised never to put
on any more.

Enter PLACIDE.

PLAC. (*unperceived, and collecting sheets of music on
piano*). The fact is, that the parlor smelled so this
morning, I was obliged to open all the windows.

TUF. Here's the other one.

BERG. That makes four.

MART. (*rising*). Have you come here again?

PLAC.* Why, now that you've got out of your light-
ning-rod (*takes tongs away from* BERGERIN) —

MART. Didn't I discharge you? — say.

PLAC. Oh, yes! These twenty years you have dis-
charged me every morning; but I haven't gone off much
for all that.

MART. (*to* TUF. *and* BERG.) Well, what do you
think of her?

PLAC. A pretty kettle of fish! As if I didn't know
better than you what you want. I should just like to see
you find my fellow.

MART. I don't doubt.

PLAC. I think I see myself leaving you. No, no! the
goat must browse where she's tied.

MART. (*furious*). Well, browse, but hold your
tongue.

PLAC. Because I refused to shut the door on Mr.
Cæsar.

* Bergerin, Placide, Marteau, Marion, Mad. Tuffier, Lucie, Tuffier.

MAD. TUF. (*who has been off wool-gathering, hears the last word*). Cæsar! has he come back?

MART. Yes, the puppy!

MAD. TUF. (*turning over pamphlet*). Ah! I'm very glad. .

MART. (*astonished*). Why so?

MAD. TUF. He must be covered with mud.

MART. What? (*General surprise.*) .

TUF. (*aside.*) Good! Now she thinks it's the porter's dog.

MAD. TUF. Isn't he grateful? He always remembers that I pulled out that bone that stuck in his throat.

MART. You pulled a bone out of my nephew's throat!

MAD. TUF. (*rising*). Oh! you're talking about your nephew, are you?

MART. I should imagine so.

MAD. TUF. (*comes down*). Well, Heaven bless you!

TUF. It does need some patience.

MAD. TUF. You annoy me; you —

LUC. Poor Madame Tuffier!

MAD. TUF. I say, I say, my little chit, this tone of commiseration don't please me at all (*goes up, and sits on sofa*).

LUC. O madame! I hope you don't imagine —

PLAC.* Here's the question, ma'am. Monsieur Marteau wants me to turn away Mr. Cæsar.

MAD. TUF. (*not listening*). I'm pretty old; but I don't drivel yet.

PLAC. A fine young man, so gentlemanly!

MAD. TUF. And, after all, it isn't everybody who can arrive at my age, and —

PLAC. And that in order to let in a Monsieur Tiburce.

---

* Bergerin, Marion, Marteau, Placide, Ma'l. Tuffier, Lucie, Tuffier.

MAD. TUF. I've got good eyes, good legs —   ◢

PLAC. An idiot!

MART. (*to* PLAC.) Hold your tongue!

MAD. TUF. (*furious, rises*). Who dares order me to hold my tongue?

MART. (*screams*). No, no! it's —

PLAC. Oh, well! if you won't hear me — (*Goes up.*)

MAD. TUF. What's that? The very servant insults me.

PLAC. I?

TUF. (*exasperated*). Oh, oh, oh!

MART. (*ditto*). Enough to make one jump out of window.

MAD. TUF. I'm going; good-by! And I'll never darken these doors again. (*Exit.*)

MAR. *and* LUC. Madame!

TUF. (*alarmed*). Don't stop her. Oh! I'm just done up. (*Falls into chair*, R.)

PLAC. It's your Mr. Tiburce who has done it all.

LUC. Certainly: with his vanilla.

MART. (*to* MAR.) Don't listen to them, Marion: they want to influence you. He's a charming fellow. He'll leave off his hair-oil, and you'll be perfectly happy. You know I only desire your happiness; don't you?

MAR.* But I tell you again, papa, I don't love him.

MART. You will love him, my darling, without his hair-oil: you'll see you will. Only think, — a man who can cut a cork without screaming. Why, you can make any thing of him you please.

MAR. (*aside*). You sha'n't make a husband for me of him, any way! (*Ring in vestibule.*)

BERG. Here's Tiburce.

LUC. (*half aloud*). Whew! I smell the vanilla.

---

* Bergerin, Placide, and Lucie higher up; Marion, Marteau, Tuffier.

Plac. (*aloud*). Nasty; ain't it? (*Exit into dining-room.*)

Mart. Silence! (*To* Marion.) Treat him well, now, for the sake of your adopted father.

Berg. (*on threshold, announces*). Monsieur Tiburce Ratisson!

Mart.* Come in, my dear sir; come in! The ladies were just talking of you.

Mar. (*to* Luc. *at a distance*). He's a fright.

Luc. (*ditto*). Perfect fright.

Tib. (*bows*). You are very good, ladies.

Luc. Sir!

Mar. Sir! Come, let's go and pacify Madame Tuffier. (*Exeunt, with handkerchiefs at nose.*)

Mart. Ah! I'd just as lief they'd be gone. Now, young man, let's sit down and talk seriously, — if we can. (*All sit.*)† In the first place, you told Monsieur Bergerin that you were coming this morning.

Tib. Yes, sir.

Mart. Very good. Is it to retract, after yesterday's scene?

Tib. (*rises*). O sir!

Mart. (*makes him sit*). You're still in the same mind, then?

Tib. More than ever (*rises*).

Mart. (*makes him sit*). Very good. I congratulate you. It was to be feared that your going off with my nephew might lead to something.

Tuf. In the excited state you both were in; for, as for him —

Berg. How he treated us!

---

* Marion, Marteau, Tiburce, and Bergerin at back; Lucie, Tuffier.
† Tiburce, Bergerin, Marteau, Tuffier.

Tuf. (*rising*). Treated us like dogs.

Berg. (*ditto*). Rather like cats.

Mart. When you've done —

Tuf. Go on, go on!

Tib. Yes, yes: the truth is, he was rather on his high horse; and I was on mine too.

Berg., Mart., Tuf. (*anxiously*). Yes?

Tib. Oh, yes! It happened just as you might suppose.

All Three (*anxious*). Ah!

Tib. I demanded the explanation of his conduct.

All Three. Yes?

Tib. We got rather heated in talking, you understand; and one thing led to another, until finally —

All Three. Yes?

Tib. We went and had a supper together.

All Three (*surprised*). Ah!

Tib. Yes. Oh! he's a good fellow, — a little cracked, but so jolly! He made me laugh well; and we separated the best of friends. We call each other by first names.

Tuf. Well, so much the better.

Berg. It's more touching.

Mart. Yes, never mind. Then he didn't say any thing to dissuade you?

Tib. Nothing.

Mart. (*rising*). Didn't your marriage seem to provoke him somewhat?

Tib. Not at all. (*Aside.*) How stupid of me not to remember! (*Aloud.*) Yes, yes: what am I saying? Yes, he was in a perfect rage, and ended by swearing that the marriage should never come off.

Mart. (*sits*). Ah! indeed. Well, we'll see about that.

Tib. (*aside*). I guess I'm sly enough for him.

Mart. We'll drop the subject of Monsieur Cæsar, and come to matters of interest; for I suppose that is what brought you here this morning.

Tib. Matters of interest? — just so.

Mart. Yes. Bergerin has told you the main point, hasn't he? — namely, that Marion is not my daughter.

Tib. But an adopted child. Yes, sir. Ah! that speaks well for your heart.

Mart. Yes: don't interrupt me. We'll say, then, an adopted child, brought up in my house like my own daughter.

Tib. I can't speak my admiration for conduct —

Mart. D—n it! Don't interrupt me.

Berg. Don't interrupt him! D—n it!

(*Draws out watch, and begins to wind.*)

Tib. No, sir.

Mart. (*provoked by noise of watch*). Has he told you time, place, and circumstances?

Tib. Not a word.

Mart. Indispensable things, nevertheless. (*Leans towards* Bergerin *to make him stop.*)

Berg. (*shows watch*). Half-past one; but I think I'm fast.

Mart. Before considering the other question —

Tib. (*having drawn out watch*). Yes: two minutes at least.

Tuf. (*ditto*) (*to* Tib.) I agree with you: that's a fact.

Berg. (*interrupting him, and rising*). Relate it to him then, my dear friend; for as for me, with my susceptible organization, you might as well ask me to act a melodrama. (*Sets his watch.*) The mere recollection thrills my nerves with horror.

(*He walks to the fireplace.*)

Tuf. (*blows his nose*). Certainly, the mere recollection —

MART. (*agacé*). Yes, of course: that's agreed to. (*To* TIBURCE) You must know then, my dear sir, that one January evening — was it January, though, or February?

TUF. February.

BERG. January.

MART. Yes, it was December; but no matter for that. In the year —

BERG. 1840.

TUF. '39.

BERG. '40.

MART. Well, '39 or '40.

BERG. '40. I was already second superintendent at the Post.

MART. Let's say '40.

TIB. Call it '40, and proceed.

MART. Then, young man —

BERG. There was snow on the ground.

TUF. And what a frost!

BERG. Why, the mercury stood at —

MART. When you've got through, say so.

BERG. Sho! what's he got now?

TUF. He's worse than ever to-day.

BERG. Oh, go on, go on! (*Walks up and down at back.*)

MART. That's lucky (*to* TIBURCE). Then, young man, we were just leaving our lawyer's, who had sent for us on the most important business. An old friend of ours had died, and left us each a considerable legacy.

BERG. (*stops in walk*). Yes, — forty thousand francs to Marteau —

MART. It is not essential to —

TUF. (*on the other side*). Twelve thousand francs to Bergerin —

MART. (*turns to* TUF.) It matters little —

5

BERG. And thirteen thousand francs to Tuffier.

MART. But, great Jupiter! —

TUF. (*to* TIB., *rising*). You'll remark that's just nineteen years ago.

MART. I —

BERG. (*to* TIB.) And we've not yet received a sou.

MART. Will you —

TUF. (*to* TIB.) Still they go on giving us hopes from one day to another, —

(MARTEAU *rises, takes* TUFFIER *by the collar, and sets him down on his chair.*)

TUF. (*screams*). Well, well! (BERGERIN, *frightened, sits on piano-stool.*)

MART. It's enough to drive one mad!

TIB. Calm yourself.

MART. (*waits a moment*). Ah! at last. (*Resuming.*) Then, young man, we were just leaving —

BÉRG. You've said that already.

MART. (*rises, as though to fall on* BERGERIN, *but sits again, nearer* TIBURCE, *on the chair left by* BERGERIN. TIBURCE *begins to swing his foot*). Oh! (*Resumes.*) I stop in the rue Lafitte to light a cigar in the corner of a doorway; and suddenly I hear at my feet (*stops* TIBURCE'S *foot*) the cry of a child. I stoop, I see a cradle, and within an infant in swaddling-clothes. I call these gentlemen. Inspired by his excellent heart, Bergerin proposed to hand over the child to the porter, and Tuffier to carry it to the police-station. The last motion was carried. Therefore we repaired to the commissary's, and made our statement in form. The child was a girl; and, without adjournment, I proposed to these gentlemen to adopt it on the spot.

TIB. All three of you?

MART. All three of us. Whereupon, brother Tuffier commences to cry out, "Murder —

Tuf. I should think so, by Jove! — with a wife and a child. (*Sits in chair left by* Marteau.)

Mart. And Bergerin to make his lamentations —

Berg. (*rising, to* Tib.) I who have to deny myself the one for fear of having the other. (*Passes to fireplace.*)

Mart. (*to* Tib.) Well, here we are again. It was just this enthusiasm then. When I saw What's-his-name pretending his wife's anxiety, Bergerin gaping in his chair, and the child crying on the table, — by George! it touched me. It's true, it did! — the little darling, with its cunning little hands all red with cold, left like a bundle. I thought of my little Lucie quietly asleep in her chamber. I imagined her shivering in the snow at night under people's feet. My heart was pierced, and I began to weep like a beast. I took the baby under my arm, and carried it to the house, squeezing it as if it had been my own.

Tuf. A beautiful impulse!

Berg. (*warming his feet*). Yes, indeed.

Mart. There we were in the street again —

Berg. (*recommences to walk up and down at back*). Ah! I sha'n't forget that night in a hurry. Not a cab, and a bitter cold —

Mart. (*annoyed by* Bergerin's *walking*). A snapping cold, yes, which brightened up my ideas; so much so, that, while walking with the cradle under my arm, — (*Looks at* Bergerin.) He's going to begin again. These gentlemen behind me like a christening procession. I began to make some mental calculations. "Come, let's see. I take the child; very well. I pay for every thing, and undertake the whole; good: but, when she's grown up, who will provide her portion?"

Tib. (*ceasing to weep*). What's that? (*Pockets his handkerchief.*)

MART. Who will give her a dowry?

BERG. Yes: who is to give her a dowry?

MART. You see, the cares were already beginning. An idea struck me. I turn, and say to Bergerin, " I say, are you going to leave me the entire charge of the child — you two, — are you actually as hard-hearted as that ? "

BERG. (*comes down*, R.) Hard-hearted! I was crying more than he was. (*Sits on chair at extreme right.*)

MART. (*sits on sofa*). With cold, yes. Now, here was what I proposed, and they accepted (prick up your ears, young man), — to buy a strong box, a real one, you know, of iron.

TIB. Yes.

MART. With three different locks, and, consequently, three keys.

TIB. Yes.

MART. One for each of us; for fear of any indiscretion.

TIB. Yes.

MART. And by an opening arranged in the top of the said box — like the savings banks — to contribute all three what each could economize, taking one year with another — one more and one less — just as we chose, without any control: so that we should only have to open it when Marion should be of age, to be provided for, and when we should all agree on the choice of a husband. Do you understand? (*Rises.*)

TIB. (*rises*). A money-box!

MART. (*opening the top of the chiffonier, and showing the box fastened into the wood*). Which is here.

TIB. Ah!

MART. And which has had some time to fill up in eighteen years.

TIB. (*knocking on box*). Then Mademoiselle Marion's dowry is in here?

ALL. Yes. (TUFFIER *rises*.)

TIB. And for the future you don't bind yourself?

MART. (*takes his hand*). To die in two years. No, young man, I can't do that for you. Now, will you marry, or won't you marry?

TIB. (*pressing* TUF.'s *hand*). Oh! I'll marry, I'll marry; but let's open first.*

MART. On the spot; and we'll settle all without adjournment.

ALL. Very good (*all three feel in pockets*).

CÆS. (*opening window, and speaking from garden*). Very good; and, if the amount don't suit Monsieur Tiburce, Monsieur Tiburce is your very humble servant, and you have your labor for your pains.

MART. He again!

CÆS. Oh! I warned you. By the window this time (*jumps into room*); and I dare say just in time, too, to prevent your making a blunder.

TUF. (*stops* MART., *and calls* BERG.) Stop — here — I say, though, it strikes me your nephew's right. If the dowry don't suit him, then good-evening. †

BERG. He won't marry. (*Goes to sit on sofa*.)

CÆS.‡ And the spell is broken. Old gentlemen, you are still pretty young for your age.

TUF. Then we won't open at all. (*Goes up*.)

TIB. How's that, how's that? Then where's the dowry? She hasn't any, now.

CÆS.§ One word, my son. Do you marry the young lady, or the money?

---

* Marteau, Tiburce, Tuffier, Bergerin.
† Marteau, Tuffier, Bergerin, Cæsar, Tiburce.
‡ Bergerin, Marteau, Cæsar, Tuffier, Tiburce.
§ Bergerin, Tuffier, Marteau, Cæsar, Tiburce.

5*

Tib.   Why, both.

Cæs.   Which by choice?

Tib. (*embarrassed*).   Why, the young lady.

Cæs.   Then marry her.   We'll open the bank afterwards. (*Goes up.*)

Tib.   How do you expect me to marry without seeing
the money?

Mart.   He hesitates.

Tib.   D—d fool!

Mart. (*turning his back on him*).   Candidate rejected.

Tib.   Why need he have come in just now?

Mart.   As for you —   (*Moves toward* Cæsar.)

Cæs. (*taking his hand*).   Oh, don't thank me! —
there's no occasion, — only give me some breakfast: I'm
hungry as a wolf. (*Rings.*)

Mart. (*starts back*).   Breakfast!

Enter Placide.

Plac. (*enters from dining-room*).   Mr. Cæsar!

Cæs. (*seated at table*).   Coffee, quick!

Plac.   Right away! (*To* Marteau.)   You see he did
get in. (*Runs back into dining-room.*)

Mart.   Well, we are going to see how he'll get out.
My coat, quick! (*Takes off dressing-gown.*)

Tib. (*runs to him.*)*   But, Monsieur Marteau —

Mart.   Well, what have you got to say?   I'll give you
one hour to decide.

Tib.   One hour!

Mart.   No more; and if you don't give me your word
then and here to marry without regard to the money —

Tib.   And suppose I do give it to you?

Mart.   Before witnesses, very good: then we'll open.

* Bergerin, Tuffier, Marteau, Tiburce, Cæsar.

Cæs. (*arranging table for breakfast*). Well, and suppose he gives his word, and takes it back afterwards?

Tuf. That's been seen.

Berg. Let him try. I'll have him turned out of the post-office.

Mart. And I'll give him a thrashing.

Tib. Thank you.

Mart. Is that understood?

Tib. I should think so.

Mart. (*looks at watch*). You have till two o'clock to make your decision.

Tib. The devil!

Plac. (*enters with breakfast on waiter, and coat tucked under her arm*). There's your coat.

Mart. (*takes coat angrily*). Is that the way to bring a coat? (*To* Cæsar.) As to you, sir —

Cæs. (*sitting down to eat*). Good appetite, eh? Thank you.

Mart. (*with dignity*). I propose to inquire at the police-station whether you have a right to break into my house.

Cæs. (*quietly*). You know where it is, I suppose, — the police-station. Third street to the left as you go up; a red lantern over the door.

Mart. (*taking cane*). Oh! (*Goes to door.*)

Tib. (*stops him, and begs*). Monsieur Marteau, just give me till to-morrow.

Mart. (*pushes him off*). Oh! let me alone you! This fellow's always getting under my feet. (*Exit, making* Tiburce *spin round.*)

Tib. Monsieur Marteau, Monsieur Marteau! (*Aside.*) I'd better go and consult my lawyer, — Monsieur Marteau, Monsieur Marteau! (*Exit, running.*)

Cæs. (*aside*). It's for us three to settle now; and I

vow to God, Uncle Marteau, you sha'n't open your money-box so easy as you think (*coffee-pot in hand*). Come, gentlemen. Coffee must be taken hot.

TUF. What?

BERG. (*rising*). Coffee for us!

CÆS. Ah, Monsieur Tuffier! you won't refuse me that?

TUF.* Oh! thank you. It would keep me awake for a week.

BERG. So it would me. I have to forego it, — another self-denial caused by my unhappy nerves.

CÆS. (*cup in hand, seated*, R.) Do you know it must be terrible to have such organizations?

BERG. Oh! don't speak of it.

TUF. A life of self-denial, when one might enjoy every thing.

BERG. With a pretty fortune too. Oh! it would be far better to be poor —

TUF. And not have any nerves.

CÆS. Then you could enjoy your coffee when you pleased.

TUF. Yes, indeed!

CÆS. Only you would have nothing to buy it with.

TUF. (*surprised*). True.

BERG. (*ditto*). That's so! (*Aside.*) Why, he has a way of reasoning things out — this fellow. (CÆSAR *gives him cup.* BERGERIN, *astonished passes it to* TUFFIER, *who puts it on table.*)

CÆS. Well, one can't expect every thing in this world.

TUF. *and* BERG. No.

CÆS. (*rising*). For instance, I haven't any thing.

TUF. That's rather slim.

* Cæsar, Bergerin, Tuffier.

Cæs. But I'm well and hearty, while Monsieur Bergerin — now there's a man who has — how much? Twenty to twenty-five thousand francs income?

Berg. Oh! twenty thousand at the very highest.

Cæs. And for himself alone.

Berg. Alas! for myself alone.

Cæs. You'll reply to that, that I don't own like him a grand suite of apartments big enough for an English family, with the duty of promenading there alone with a candle in order to look at my tongue in every mirror. Now, I lodge up six flights; I can sit in the middle, and touch all four walls; and I can't gape in my own face in the mirrors, for twenty-five good reasons: the first is —

Berg. (*with sly air*). Wait, let me tell you. I bet I know! It's because there ain't any. (*Laughs delighted with his own wit.*)

Cæs. That's it. So I have a great advantage over him.

Berg. An advantage!

Tuf. Of being in bad lodgings.

Cæs. Yes; but I don't care for my lodgings, don't you see.

Tuf. 'Well?

Cæs. Well, I can move out whenever my landlord says so, — and rather like it.

Tuf. Well, that's a great argument! — and so can he.

Cæs. He! I defy him to.

Tuf. Well, I like that.

Cæs. He's bored to death in his great barrack: he just vegetates there. But I'll bet you he'd scream like ten peacocks if anybody asked him to leave it.

Berg. (*alarmed*). Leave my lodgings!

Cæs. What did I tell you?

Tuf. But if you are tired of them —

BERG.   I was that twenty years ago.

CÆS.   Exactly.   It's a habit that has got to be a second nature : it has gone into his blood.

BERG.   That's so : it has.   I have my easy-chair here, — don't you see? — my table there, the mantelpiece just beyond, and my bed behind.   Well, I get up; I go to my table, and get bored there ; then I come back, and am bored before the fireplace; and so on up and down, round, zigzag, in every direction, until finally I go and bewail my wretched existence in bed.   And it's a perfectly regular thing, — every day just the same.   I've got broken to suffering just so; and if I had to reverse my habits, and change my hours, and have to yawn here when I ought to be yawning there, — why, I should be on my sick-bed in less than —

CÆS. (*aside*).   I've got you already: you won't give up your key.

BERG.   Why, just thinking of it (now, I give you my word), it's affected me already.   I feel a kind of a — you know — all over.   My nerves are in such a state, I really must take a little sedative ; and if you'll allow me (*takes out little packet*) —

CÆS.   What's that ?

BERG. (*goes to fireplace, where there is an urn*).   It's camomile.

CÆS.   Camomile ?

BERG.   Yes: I always carry it about.

TUF. (*shrugs shoulders*).   Good heavens !

BERG.*   I can make it right here.   (*Sets about making his tea, and pays no further attention to what follows.*)

TUF. (*half aside to* CÆS.)   About the exciting existence of a — cockroach (*sits near* CÆSAR *on sofa*).

---

* Cæsar, Tuffier, Bergerin.

Cæs. The fruits of celibacy. Ah! it's not very gay; but a married life, now —

Tuf. Yes: the gayety of that is worth talking about.

Cæs. A wife!

Tuf. Crazy!

Cæs. A son!

Tuf. Mad!

Cæs. Oh! marry him: he'll calm down.

Tuf. Marry him? — to Marion, I suppose.

Cæs. Why not? She has every thing in her favor, — wit, beauty, and worth; and as for her dowry —

Tuf. (*with contempt*). The money-box!

Cæs. Well, nobody knows what's in it, do they?

Tuf. Why, no: that's true.

Cæs. Well, if I were in your place, I would find out at once by opening it on the sly; and I wouldn't say no decidedly to my son, unless the amount is — You understand?

Tuf. Why, why, why! now that is an idea. I'm certainly very stupid (*rises*).

Cæs. That's so.

Tuf. That's so (*looks at box*). We must see first whether —

Berg. (*examining tea*). Oh! it's too strong.

Tuf. What is?

Berg. The tea.

Tuf. (*provoked*). Oh —

Cæs. Don't mind him; he's idiotic. So you mean to wait?

Tuf. Yes; and so must these dear children. They're in love, it seems.

Cæs. Blazing!

Tuf. (*sentimentally*). Nothing will be so dear to me as their happiness, if the dowry is—

CÆS. Certainly.

TUF. But if, on the other hand, it isn't (*changing tone*) — then they may go to the devil, both of them.

CÆS. That's a truly paternal decision.

BERG. (*to himself*). Now I've got too much water.

TUF. (*turns round*). What?

CÆS. He's got too much water.

TUF. (*angrily*). What's that to me?

BERG. Oh! that's nothing: I'll put in some more camomile.

TUF. (*aside*). He is insupportable. Well, we'll meet again — and not a word to my idiot of a wife: she'd make some absurd blunder.

CÆS. Agreed.

TUF. See you again soon. (*Exit quickly.*)

CÆS. (*aside*). You won't give up your key either. Dance away, my nervous puppets: I've just got hold of all your strings (*approaches* BERGERIN). Well, Monsieur Bergerin, do you feel better?

BERG. Yes, I am calmer already. Camomile is a sovereign remedy.

Enter LOUIS.

CÆS. Indeed!

BERG. Just as I tell you (*interrupted by a sob from* LOUIS, *who has taken seat near fireplace*) (*starts*). Good God! what's that?

LOUIS (*sobbing*). Marion loves me no more (*falls into* BERGERIN'S *arms*).

BERG. Well, what of that?

CÆS. Come, come!

LOU. (*continually preventing* BERGERIN *from drinking*). Here's an hour I've been walking in the garden under her windows. I've called, screamed: not a word.

I've thrown stones against the glass (*sobs more violently*) ; I've broken three panes.

BERG. (*frightened*). Three panes! Are you sure they were hers?

LOU. Nothing would do: she didn't appear (*sobs*). She won't see me; she don't love me (*falls into* CÆSAR's *arms*).

BERG. (*aside*). Oh! I can't see him cry that way (*takes his cup, &c.*).

LOU. (*strikes on table*). But enough tears (*changing tone*).

BERG. It's a pandemonium here! I'd rather go home, and drink there (*runs out, carrying teapot*).

LOU. She's a coquette, — a girl without heart, without soul, without any thing.

(*Strikes table violently.*)

CÆS. Without any thing? — you're blinded with rage.

LOU. (*not listening*). My nerves are in such a state!

CÆS. Drink some water.

LOU. Yes, yes! (*Seizes glass convulsively.*)

CÆS. Don't eat the tumbler.

LOU. Don't fear: I'm calm now. (*Sets down glass, and breaks it.*)

CÆS. Good!

LOU. Believe in the oaths of a woman! This Marion who had sworn to me — (*Twists a fork.*)

CÆS. (*takes it from him*). He's improving the silver.

LOU. Frailty thy name is — (*Breaks plate.*)

CÆS. Now, the plates. I wouldn't advise you to set up housekeeping.

LOU. No danger: I shall die a bachelor, like that old idiot of a Bergerin, — faithless, perfidious —

CÆS. Bergerin?

6

Lou. (*shouts*).   Marion!

Cæs.   She'll think you're calling her.

Lou.   She'll be mistaken.   It's all over: I never want
to see her again, or even to know her (*jumps up*).   I'm
going to write to her.

Cæs.   Louis, Louis!

Lou. (*rings furiously, and shouts*).   Placide, Placide!
pens, ink.   Oh! there they are (*comes back to table*).

Cæs.   Come, come; calm yourself.

Lou.   Oh! I'm calm (*kicks over chair; sits*).   Now let's
write, "Mademoiselle" (*stops*)—no (*tears the sheet, crumples it, and throws it away*).   "Ungrateful,"—no, not that
(*crumples and throws away sheet as before*).   "Little
monster!"—no, nor that either (*same play*)—no! a
thousand times no!   I won't write to her. (*Scatters to
the wind the rest of the quire.*)

Cæs.   Great Jove! what a slaughter!

Lou. (*striding about*).   I'll hunt down that Tiburce
if he hides in the bowels of the earth.   Tiburce that beast
whom she prefers to me,—I'll find him; and we'll cut
each other's throats.

Plac. (*enters*).   Lordy-massy!   ·

Lou.   Go to the devil!

Plac.   What would master say if he came home?

Lou.   What he chooses.   Master be d—d!   I hate him
too, like his daughter, his Marion, and you.   I detest you
all (*falls on chair*).   O Marion, Marion!

Plac. (*alarmed*).   He's going to faint.   Water—quick!
(*Goes for the pitcher.*)

Lou. (*rising*).   The water; yes, the water: that's it.
(*To* Placide.)   Adieu!   Give her this last kiss. (*Kisses
her.*)

Plac.   Halloo!

Lou.   I'm about to throw myself into the river. (*Exit.*)

Plac.   Ah! great heavens!

Enter MARION *and* LUCIE.

MAR. *and* LUC. What has happened?

PLAC. Mr. Louis going to drownd hisself.

MAR. Ah!

LUC. Heavens! (*They stagger.*)

CÆS. No, no! nobody's going to "drownd hisself."

MAR. (*crying*). Yes, yes: I'm sure of it. Ah! I feel I'm going off.

LUC. So am I. (*Each falls on chair.*)

CÆS. (*runs from one to the other*). Marion, Lucie! it's spreading fast. (*Slaps* MARION's *hands, and kisses* LUCIE.)

TIB. (*enters with bouquet*). My lawyer won't be back till by and by, and, in the mean time —

PLAC.* Ah! you've come, have you? Behold your work!

TIB. My work!

LOU. (*comes back*). I wasn't mistaken this time. I saw him come in, — yes. Ah! at last, I've got you.

TIB. Sir!

LOU. You've got to fight me.

TIB. (*alarmed*). Not a bit of it.

LOU. (*shakes him*). Ah, coward! Ah, wretch!

CÆS. (*separating them*). Here, here —

TIB. (*running round table*). Help, help!

LOU. (*after him*). Just let me catch him.

TIB. Watch! Police! Murder! (*Gains door, and escapes:* LOUIS *after him, and* CÆSAR *after* LOUIS.)

CÆS. Louis, Louis!

PLAC. Miss Lucie! Miss Marion! Well, here's a fine kettle of fish!

* Marion, Placide, Tiburce, Cæsar, Louis.

END OF ACT II.

ACT III.

THE SAME SCENE.

Furniture displaced; the table in front, L.; the sofa in front of fireplace; a chair to right of table; one behind sofa; another in front, R.

As curtain rises, Lucie *sits,* L., *near table, smelling salts;* Placide *stands at her side;* Marion, *seated on sofa;* Cæsar *before her, against mantelpiece.*

Cæs. (*takes glass of eau-sucré from* Marion). Well, feel a little better?

Mar. Yes.

Plac. (*to* Luc.) All over now?

Luc. All over.

Cæs. You can do it pretty well, too, when you set about it.

Mar. (*rising*). You are sure he hasn't gone to throw himself in the water?

Cæs. Perfectly. He may possibly have thrown Tiburce in, however.

Mar. (*with feeling*). Oh! That I don't care for in the least. (*Sits.* Placide *arranges things at back.*)

Cæs. I say, you do love your Louis pretty well; don't you?

Mar. My Louis! He's not mine so much as that comes to.

Luc. (*goes to the piano to take her worsted-work*).

You needn't think I am going to marry Monsieur Tiburce.

MAR. If you flatter yourself that I'll marry him any more than you —

PLAC. (*goes to* MAR.) Ah! take care, ma'amselle: you know master's very obstinate when he takes any thing into his head.

MAR. And what am I, I should like to know? In the first place, I've decided perfectly what I'll do if they undertake to force me to marry Monsieur Tiburce Ratisson.

LUC. (*coming down with embroidery*). How can anybody call themselves Ratisson?

MAR. I'll let them make all the preparations, and seem to have made up my mind to it. I'll be very sweet to Monsieur Tiburce; and then, when monsieur the mayor says to me, with all his scarfs and things, "Ma'amselle Marion, do you take Monsieur Ratisson, here present, for your wedded husband? I'll just say (*courtesy*), "No, sir." (*They come forward.*)

CÆS. There's for you!

MAR.* Well?

CÆS. You'll not have to take that trouble, I hope.

MAR. You hope, you hope? Besides, you promised to rid me of Monsieur Tiburce; and I don't see that you do it a bit.

CÆS. Patience!

LUC. We want you to hurry up about it.

MAR. And turn him out of doors right away.

LUC. Or sooner.

CÆS.† Let's see —

---

* Lucie, Marion, Cæsar, Placide, at back.
† Lucie, Cæsar, Marion, Placide, at back.

6*

MAR. (*not listening*). You came in like a man going to take command and run the whole machine.

LUC. I shall do this, and I shall do that.

MAR. And, after all, what have you done?

LUC. Yes, let's hear: what have you done?

CÆS. Well, I've breakfasted.

LUC. That's something to be proud of.

CÆS. (*strikes on his breeches pocket*). Well, I don't know about that. At any rate, you can be easy: whether he backs out or not, you sha'n't be his wife. I did mean to cure up all the nerves in the house; but now I've got another plan. I intend now, on the contrary, to aggravate them all to such a point that they'll all go crazy.

LUC. Crazy! Well, what then?

CÆS. Then we'll send them all to the asylum. That'll be a good way to get rid of them.

(PLACIDE *goes up the stage.*)

MAR. (*pouts*). Oh! you're always making fun.

CÆS. And you don't feel very funny, because Mr. Louis hasn't come back, — hey?

MAR. Well, yes, there! He is gone off angry, no doubt.

CÆS. Perhaps it's a little bit your fault too.

MAR. (*turns upon him*). My fault!

CÆS. (*recoils*). Well, don't eat me; but it would appear that last night —

MAR.* I should like to see how you'd behave if you think it's amusing to wait for somebody a whole week, and then, when they come, and you feel happy, to be just reproached, and called names (*nearly crying*). Well, that's what I go through every day.

---

* Lucie (seated), Cæsar, Marion, Placide (seated on causeuse).

Cæs. You wait a week for him every day! Why poor thing, that's terrible!

Mar. No, no! What a tease he is! (*Begins to laugh while crying, and hides her face on* Cæsar's *shoulder*).

Cæs. Aren't we a little nervous too? (*Strokes her hair.*) There, there, little pussy-cat.

Luc. How silly to give way like that!

Mar. I can't help it: it's too much for me — there!

Cæs. Let's see: do you know what you ought to do, Mariette, when he comes determined on a quarrel?

Mar. (*raises head, and wipes her eyes*). Yes, come: what should I do?

Cæs. Just receive his ill-humor without doing him the honor to take the slightest notice of it; and in three lessons I'll promise it'll be a dead calm.

Mar. Yes; but suppose it's too calm.

Cæs. Well, I only tell you the best way, — the one I shall recommend to Lucie, if ever I take it into my head to be nervous and quarrelsome after she is my wife. (*Crosses to* Lucie, *and is about to kiss her;* Marion *stoops over to look;* Cæsar *stops.*) Well?

Mar. All right! I'll go along.

(*Goes up toward* Placide.)

Cæs. (*to* Luc.) My little cousin will be my wife; won't she?

Luc. (*playing with her work*). Why —

Cæs. (*kissing her forehead*). Come, say it's a bargain, Mademoiselle Lucie, and you shall be happy: I'll swear it! My dear little girl, I know I ought to have made more of a mystery and a ceremony of it; but after all you see, between relations — so I began to love you first like a darling little sister, then like a charming little cousin, then as a lovely young girl; and now here I am beginning to love you as the one whom I must make my wife. It has come on little by little, day by day, without my thinking of it. It's unromantic, every day, and vulgar, I know; but there it is, it exists. So much so, that if you were to say, "I have reflected, cousin, and seriously decide that the answer must be no — well, then (*affected*) — absurd for a man to cry — but there it is.

Luc. (*quickly*). But it's yes, it's yes!

Cæs. (*wipes a tear*). Well, no matter: it must come out. (*Changing tone.*) It's all that little girl's fault with her nerves.

Mar. I!

Plac. Oh, yes! ma'amselle you're nervous decidedly.

Cæs. (*laughs*). It's catching beyond a doubt. Come, my little dears, we must come to an understanding.*

Luc. *and* Mar. Yes!

Cæs. Papa'll be back soon: he's gone after the myrmidons of law to arrest me.

Luc. *and* Mar. Oh! Good Heavens!

Cæs. But I defy them. As for you — whatever happens, and even during my punishment, be sweet, obedient, and affectionate, and consent to every thing.

Mar. Even to marry Tiburce?

Cæs. Yes, both of you: until I turn him out. But Uncle Marteau ought to be back by this time: the police-station isn't so far.

Plac. Ah! true, you don't know. I forgot to tell you.

Cæs. Well, tell us!

Plac. I heard it from M. Tuffier's housekeeper, — her master Monsieur Marteau and Monsieur Bergerin received a notification two hours ago from their man of business.

---

* Placide, Lucie, Cæsar, Marion.

— you know the one who had charge of that legacy affair.

Cæs. Yes, I know.

Plac. Well, he notified them that the money was at their disposition, and they had only to call at his office to get it.

Cæs. (*rising*). Somehow people don't write me such letters.

Plac. The fact is, some folks have the devil's own luck. (*Walks up stage.*)

Cæs. They'll come back here all three, pockets all stuffed out with bankbills. If that would only calm their nerves. But no — I forgot: that wouldn't do us any good; for I stick to my idea of driving them all mad.

Luc. (*looks out of window*). Cæsar, I see papa: he's coming this way.

Cæs. Good! we must dissemble. Behold the tyrant! (*Sits, l., and pretends to read paper.*)

Enter Marteau.

Mart. (*without seeing them*). What'll you have? (*Puts hat on chiffonier; hat falls; he picks it up.*) What'll you have? (*Same play: kicks away hat, and puts down cane so that it falls and rolls. Furious.*) Every thing is destroyed now, no more law, no more justice. (Placide *picks up hat;* Marion, *cane; and exit* Placide *with both.*) Here's a commissary, a magistrate whose mission it is to enforce respect for property, and to protect families; and, when I talk to him of arresting this rascal who breaks into my house like a burglar, answers me, " O Monsieur Marteau! think better of it — Your own nephew — we can't undertake to interfere in these matters." Then in what matters do you interfere, pusillanimous and shuffling magistrate? when do you interfere? (*Turns, and sees* CÆSAR *holding newspaper before his face, and chatting with the girls.*) Oh! He's there still. (*Advances slowly towards* CÆSAR, *dumb show and by-play of* MARION *and* LUCIE, *who see him coming: he slowly pulls down paper.*)

CÆS. Coop — found him now! (MARION *and* LUCIE *run back.*)

MART. So you've installed yourself and taken possession of my house in spite of me: you've breakfasted here, you'll dine and doubtless sleep here too.

CÆS. I shall sleep here certainly, uncle, so as to be able to attend you in the night, you know — a crisis might come on. (*Rises.*)

MART.* And you propose to continue this?

CÆS. Until you have recovered, and are prudent and calm as a father of a family should be, and ready to listen to my advice.

MART. Which is?

CÆS. You know well enough, to put an end to Tiburce's matrimonial pretensions.

MART. Oh! perfectly.

CÆS. And to bestow Marion's hand on my friend Louis.

MART. Because?

CÆS. Because they love each other.

MART. A fine reason certainly.

MAR. (*coming down*). But, papa, it seems to me —

MART. What do you say, miss? — it seems to you?

CÆS. Why, yes, certainly: it seems to her that that would be more logical than to give her to another on the pretext that they don't love each other.

MART. And what a choice! — an assassin who kills everybody.

* Cæsar, Marteau, Marion, Lucie, on causeuse.

MAR. But, papa, since they don't die of it —

LUC. Since they don't die of it —

MART. A debauchee, who spends all he's got.

CÆS. Oh, get out! He hasn't even got what he spends.

MART. A perfect fire-eater; fizzing off all the time, and who puts my nerves into a state —

CÆS. Well, what's the objection if he does?

MART. What's the objection!

CÆS. He isn't going to marry you.

MART.* That would be the last touch. No, he's not going to marry me; but, if I want to see Marion, I shall have to see him too, and I should be in a continual irritation.

CÆS. That don't affect Marion: what the devil! One doesn't consult his nerves on a question of son-in-law, like the barometer on a question of umbrella.

MART. Enough, incendiary. You would incite my daughters to rebel, would you? and to despise my authority. But you'll not succeed: they'll obey their father; for they've been well brought up. (MARION *and* LUCIE *go up and turn their backs.*) Won't you, Marion, obey your papa Marteau?

MAR. Why, yes; that is, if —

CÆS. If you order her to marry her lover.

MART.† Never!

CÆS. Oh! come, uncle, now for a good impulse. Say yes, and put into Mariette's money-box that great fat pocket-book that ruins the set of your coat. (*Touches his pocket.*)

MART. Hey — what?

CÆS.‡ Certainly, that great lump: it's awfully ugly.

---

* Cæsar, Marteau, Marion (seated on causeuse), Lucie (standing).

† Cæsar, Lucie, Marion, at back; Marteau.

‡ Lucie, Marion, at back; Marteau, Cæsar.

Mart. So, you are spying, and meddling with my affairs, are you?

Cæs. Why, it's no secret.

Mart. And you presume to dispose of my property in that way?

Cæs. Good God! No. Keep your property, and give us our lovers.

Luc. *and* Mar. Yes, yes!

Mart. This devil of a Louis. (*Violent ring ; jumping up.*) There! I've no need of asking who rung then.

Mar. Nor I, — it's he (*joyfully*).

Mart. And I am to introduce into my family a fellow who announces himself in that way, — never! It's a question of life or death for me. (*Another ring.*) Why, the madman would shatter me, like a pane of glass.

Cæs. For all that, he must marry Marion.

Mart.* For all that, Marion shall marry Tiburce; and here on the spot, now. The lawyer is coming, and the other gentlemen; and we shall open the box, and — I'm going to get my key — Pirate!

Cæs. Go, and get it, corsair! (Marteau *enters his room ;* Louis *appears, bell-pull in hand, with melancholy air.*)

Mar. (*aside*). Here he is.

Cæs. (*taking bell-pull*). You pursue, then, your devastating track.

Lou. (*calm*). I don't know how that happened: I hardly rang. (*Goes to sit down,* L.)

Cæs. Yes, so it seems.

Mar. (*to* Cæs.)† How strange he appears!

Luc. How calm he is!

Mar. He must be ill.

---

* Marteau, Cæsar, Marion, at door at back ; Lucie.

† Louis, Marion, Cæsar, Lucie.

Cæs. (*laughs*). It's the prostration which always follows a great crisis; the opposite extreme which nervous people always undergo. (*To* Lucie.) By George! I never thought of that.

Lou. (*rising*). Miss Lucie, Miss Marion, I have come to ask your pardon, most humbly for the scandalous scene which I just now —

Mar. Oh! there's no harm done.

Lou. Yes, yes! I was wrong, and I have acknowledged it even before Monsieur Tiburce.

Luc. Bah!

Lou. My mother explained to me, that —

Cæs. Oh! Mother Tuffier is going to set it straight: we're all right now. (*Goes up.*)

Lou. After all, Monsieur Tiburce only demands his rights, since he has your father's consent, and perhaps yours.

Mar. Mine!

Luc. (*to* Cæs.) What does he say?

Lou. I have come therefore to bid you farewell forever. (*Goes for his hat on table.*)

Mar. (*taking away hat, so that he can't get it*). What!

Cæs. (*seated on sofa*). Good, now! what did I tell you?

Mar. (*to* Lou.) Monsieur Tiburce has my consent, did you say?

Lou. (*mournfully*). Oh! I don't blame you, Marion.

Mar. But —

Lou. (*not listening*). You are not your own mistress.

Mar. I —

Lou. You don't belong to yourself, under the circumstances.

Mar. Why, I tell you again —

7

Lou. And then this man, if he has won your affection —

Luc. *and* Mar. But —

Lou. I must respect him; for he can be no ordinary character who has gained Marion's love.

Mar. But don't I tell you —

Lou. (*turning towards her*). You would, perhaps, do violence to your feelings.

Mar. But I tell you again —

Lou. There is no necessity. Should you return to me, it would doubtless be through compassion.

Mar. Eh!

Lou. And my heart demands no charity. I desire not your pity.

Mar. (*provoked*). Well, now look here —

Lou. Oh! At least, Marion, you should not abuse me. Spare me your bitter words.

Mar. Mine!

Lou. Since I do justice upon myself in withdrawing — since I restore you your liberty.

Mar. (*excited*). I can't help it; I'm going off. Now for this one last time —

Lou. (*extends hand, without looking at her*). Yes: give me your hand, Marion, for the last time.

Mar. My hand!

Lou. The hand to which I had the audacity to aspire.

Mar. Oh, my nerves! my nerves!

Lou. Let me carry away, at least, this memory in my wretched exile. (*Throws himself in* Cæsar's *arms*.)

Mar. (*bursts out in nervous paroxysm, and beats him with all her might*). There! if you want my hand, there it is for you.

Lou. Why, what's got into her? (*Runs away,* Marion *after him, striking*.)

Mar. Stop! There's for your eternal farewell, and that for your Tiburce, and that for your compassion and your charity and your magnanimity. (*Falls exhausted on seat.*) There, that's done me good ! *

Cæs. (*laughs*). Well, you deserve it.

Lou. (*throws himself at* Marion's *knees.*) † Great God, then, you love me still !

Mar. (*raising her hand*). Have you any more doubts ?

Lou. (*raising hands to parry*). No more, no more.

Mar. (*falling back, seated*). Oh, so much the better : I'm rather fatigued.

Cæs. Oh, there's no doubt about it ! There should be a water-cure here, and cold douches always ready.

Lou. (*rising*). Well, Mr. Tiburce — well, idiot, — she don't love you; and, what's more, she can't abide you, you brute : so there's your little account settled.

Cæs. (*laughs*). He's coming to himself again.

Lou. (*To* Mar.) If he doesn't renounce all pretensions to marrying you, I'll strangle him.

Cæs. All right (*picks up bell-pull*) ; and here's just what you'll need to do it with.

Lou. (*puts it in his pocket without noticing it*). Thank you ! I shall wait a few minutes. I want to see how it is ; I shall be perfectly calm.

Cæs.‡ Ah ! I always rely upon you for that.

Lou. But when the whole affair is arranged, and he has accepted —

Cæs. (*makes gesture of strangling*). Couic ! that's understood. But hush ! here's the victim !

Mar. (*rising*). My father !

---

* Louis, Marion, Cæsar, Lucie.
† Marion, Louis, Cæsar, Lucie.
‡ Marion seated, Louis, Cæsar, Lucie.

Luc. (*looks out of window*). And the other gentlemen?

Cæs. Run away, my little kittens, and rely on me:
I'll watch over your happiness.

Mar. Thank you!

Lou. And you really love me?

Mar. Again? Take that! (*Boxes his ears, and runs
off with* Lucie, *in her room.*)

Lou. Oh, how happy I am!

Cæs. The matter's settled now, you know. (*Makes
sign of fighting.*)

Lou. Oh, that's all one to me!

Cæs. I'm sure it is to me (*seeing the others*). Here
they are. Lovers, stand to your guns. (Bergerin *and*
Tuffier *enter at back;* Marteau, *from his chamber.*)

Berg. (*to* Mart. *with satisfaction.*) I say, you've got
yours; haven't you? (*Shows pocket-book.*)

Mart.* (*with ill humor*). Yes, yes, but —

Tuf. So have we (*slaps pocket-book in his pocket,
and rubs his hands*). After to-morrow, some nice little
investment —

Berg. I know one at ten per cent.

Mart. But, Good Heavens! that's not our bu-iness
now, but the other. The lawyer is here; he's drawing
the contract, and — (*Looks round.*) Well, where the
devil is Tiburce?

Tib. (*who has been a minute on threshold, hesitating to
enter*). Here I am! here I am!

Mart. Ah! (*To* Tuffier *and* Bergerin.) You've
got your keys?

Tuf. (*hesitates*). I believe so.

Berg. Mine should be in my vest-pocket.

Mart. All right. Now sit down, everybody.

---

* Marteau, Bergerin, Tuffier, Cæsar, Louis at fireplace.

Tib. (*aside*). I don't like the little fire-eater being h re. Still, if he was sincere just now —

Mart. (*to* Tib.)* Well, it's for you to speak.

Tib. Monsieur, after having conferred with my lawyer —

Mart. Ah! come to the point.

Tib. Decided by his advice —

Mart. (*rising*). You don't marry.

Tib. (*rising*). I do marry. (Louis *starts.* Cæsar *holds him.*)

Mart. You do marry, without seeing?

Tib. Eyes shut.

All (*surprised*). Ah!

Mart. (*rising*). Good! You're less mean than I supposed. Give us your hand; and since you've passed your word, and the affair is settled, we will open at once, and sign the contract afterwards, without adjournment (*turning to* Cæsar), in order to spite this gentleman.

Cæs. Oh, pshaw! I'll bet you don't open!

Mart. Really — well — you'll see in a minute. Your keys, gentlemen.

Berg. In a moment. (*Feels in his pocket.*)

Cæs. (*aside to* Tuf.) Think of your son.

Tuf. (*aside to* Cæs.) I do.

Lou. (*hardly able to contain himself, to* Cæs.) But I don't intend to allow —

Cæs. Wait a minute.

Mart. (*very nervous*). Well — The keys, the keys!

Tuf. (*standing*). Keys, keys! Seems to me you're in a great hurry. In the first place, are we going to open in public, this way, — before everybody?

Mart. Well?

* Bergerin and Marteau (seated), Tuffier (on causeuse), Tiburce (in front), Cæsar (standing at fireplace), Louis (R. on arm-chair.)

7*

Berg. Why not?

Tuf. I think it's ridiculous, for my part. We ought to do it in private, — we three.

Cæs. (*aside*). Good!

Mart. What idea has he got in his head now?

Tuf. In that way, at least, we should see — we should know —

Mart. We should see — we should know — Well, isn't it just in order to see that —

Tuf. No; but really, I think you are going too fast. You don't seem to have the real paternal feelings.

Mart. I ! — not the real paternal feelings!

Tuf. Why, no! You don't seem to suspect the real value of your little Marion; you just throw her into what's-his-name's face, as if he were the only one in the world who would take her : but there are others besides him.

Lou. (*over* Tib's *shoulder*). Yes, there's I in the first place. (Cæsar *holds him back.*)

Tib. (*turning round to* Lou.) Ah, bah! You again!

Tuf. (*to his son*). Who's talking to you? Hold your tongue !

Mart. Well, will you give your key ? — yes, or no?

Tuf. Well, no: I won't give it. There !

Cæs. (*aside to* Tuf.) Well done!

Mart. I say, do you want me to tell you what you are after now? Well, it's your boy you're manœuvring for.

Tuf. I ! — did I say the first word about my boy?

Lou. No ; and that's just where you missed it.

Tuf. (*low*). Will you hold your tongue ?

Lou. No: I won't hold my tongue.

Tib. (*to* Lou.) But what you told me just now —

Lou. It was just to humbug you.

Tib. (*rising*). Sir ! (*Crosses*, r.)

Lou. (*to his father*).* Why can't you do something

---

* Bergerin, Marteau, Tuffler, Louis, Cæsar, Tiburce.

for me? I'm your son certainly : you wouldn't cast me off —

TUF. (*low*). Have you got through, idiot?

LOU. No, I haven't got through. I have no idea of being cast off. (*To* MARTEAU.) Well, yes, there — I don't care — it is for me that he is trying to manœuvre.

TUF. But it's not true, you good-for-nothing rascal.

LOU. Yes!

TUF. No!

LOU. Yes!

TUF. Oh! that's the way, is it? (*Furious, throws* Louis *on sofa*). Well, then, there's your key, take it. Who wants your Marion !* (*Crosses, and puts key on table, then goes up.*)

CÆS. (*to* LOU.) You caught it that time.

MART. (*takes key*). At last : that makes one.

CÆS. (*aside*). Yes; but there's two more needed.

TIB. Well, now things seem to be going all right.

CÆS. I should think so.

MART. (*sneers*). I should say so, certainly. Bergerin, your key.

BERG. (*who had remained seated*). Have they finished squabbling?

MART. Yes.

BERG. Then I may be allowed —

MART. (*shakes him*). Your key.

BERG. There, there! Wait one minute. (*Feels in pockets.*)

CÆS. (*aside*). At least. (*Aloud.*) Oh! by the way, Tiburce, you know my uncle won't hear of Marion's living anywhere but here.

TIB. Oh! I'll live just where they please.

---

* Marteau, Bergerin, Tiburce, Tuffier, Louis, Cæsar.

Mart. (*to* Cæs.) What business is that of yours?

Cæs. You will have to take rooms in the house.

Mart. Will you just let us alone if you please?

Cæs. Bergerin's, I suppose.

Berg. (*jumps up*). What! my apartment?

Cæs. In the first place, there are no others.

Lou. It's the only one.

Mart. (*threatening* Cæs.) Pirate!

Berg. (*very agitated*). What! take away my second floor, and give it to him — my apartment!

Mart. Well, what then? It would break no bones.

Berg. The rooms I've lived in for twenty years? — and restored ceilings, floors, and cupboards!

Mart. Why, where would you have me put the poor children?

Berg. Put 'em down cellar if you choose. I'm satisfied where I am, and mean to stay.

Mart. (*getting excited*). You mean to stay? — you mean to stay if I choose to let you; and there's no necessity of shouting about it, either.

Berg. You'll actually have the face to warn me out?

Mart. Oh, yes! and have the notice served by a constable too.

Berg. Oh! that's the style, is it? Very good. Give me notice, and I don't give up my key. (*Puts it back in pocket.*)

Tib. Good! There we are again.

Mart. Did one ever see?

Tib. Come, come, Monsieur Bergerin.

Cæs. Yes, Monsieur Bergerin, one must be just too.

Berg. Just, just! Well, you are charming.*

---

* Bergerin, Marteau (higher up), Cæsar, Tuffier (farther up), Tiburce, Louis on causeuse.

CÆS. Oh! I'm perfectly aware that a change in habits and mode of life at your age is often dangerous.

BERG. I should think it was indeed dangerous.

LOU. It's fatal!

BERG. Fatal! He's said it: that's the word.

MART. On! go on. Blow the fire, you fillibuster!

CÆS. Still, think of these poor young people.

BERG. Let them go to the devil! Not a key do I give up without my apartment. (*Rises, and crosses to extreme* L.)

MART. Well, there! I'll leave you your apartment: there now!

CÆS. (*aside*). Murder!

LOU. Oh! d—n it!

BERG. Oh, yes!—you'd like to extract my key, and then have your notice served to-morrow.

CÆS. Just so.

MART. (*after threatening gesture to* CÆS.*) I tell you it's yours. *Sacré bleu!* what more do you want?—a lease?

BERG. Yes; for fifty years.

MART. A hundred, if you say so.

BERG. You'll have my chimneys repaired?

MART. Yes.

BERG. And paint the landing green?

MART. Yes; and you too. Any thing else?

BERG. You give me your word before witnesses?

MART. Yes.

BERG. At that price, I'll give up the key.

TIB. At last!

MART. *Ouf!*

BERG. (*feels in pockets*). Well, now: where have I stuck it?

---

* Bergerin, Tuffier (farther up), Marteau, Cæsar, Louis, Tiburce.

CÆS. (*aside to* TUF.) I say, you're the one to be turned out, then.

TUF. Why, that's a fact! (*To* MARTEAU.) I say, am I the one you propose to turn out, then? *

MART. Come! here's the other, now. Who's put that in your head?

TUF. Why — (*Points to* CÆSAR.)

MART. That serpent! — if you listen to him —

TUF. (*insisting*). But still —

MART. Well, then, I won't turn out anybody: there!

ALL. Ah!

MART. Ah! And I give the young people the pavilion with the vegetable-garden. Ah!

TUF. That means you let it to them.

MART. I don't let them any thing at all. I give it to them.

TUF. How?

MART. By deed.

TIB.† Ah, monsieur!

TUF. And the vegetable-garden too?

MART. Yes.

TUF. (*to* LOU.) There, you naughty boy! — see what you've lost.

LOU. It was your fault.

CÆS. Thunder! A two-story pavilion, and the vegetable-garden, and the money-box — there's a dowry for you.

TUF. I should think it was.

MART. Are we going to get through to-day?

·TIB. Shall we proceed?

TUF. (*stopping*). Let's see, let's see. Don't let us do things blindfold, eh! — and let's endeavor not to be nervous.

---

* Bergerin, Marteau, Tuffier, Tiburce, Louis on causeuse, Cæsar.
† Bergerin, Marteau, Tiburce, Tuffier, Louis, Cæsar.

MART. But it's you —

TUF.* Oh! it's I, it's I! You take these absurd fancies to people, and then away you go.

MART. Well.

TUF. Well — I don't know. But this fellow, — there's something underhanded about him.

TIB. What?

MART. How?

TUF. It isn't all on the square.

LOU. Very far from it.

TUF. There's some speculation about it, I want you to understand. (*Moves* TIBURCE *away*.)

BERG. (*pulls* MART. *by sleeve*). I say —

TUF. He knows there's a money-box — good. And then he gets the lodgings.

CÆS. And then there's the pavilion.

LOU. And then the vegetable-garden.

TIB. (*to* MART.) Shall we proceed?

BERG. (*to* MART.) I've thought of something.

TUF. (*to* LOU. *and* CÆS.) Why, he gets every thing; don't you see, he gets every thing.

LOU. At one fell swoop.

CÆS. Exactly.

TUF. It's ignoble!

LOU. Shameful!

CÆS. Immoral!

TUF. (*turning to* MART.) Immoral!

BERG. (*to* MART.) Suppose we make out the lease right away?

TUF. And then all the expectations, and a pretty girl thrown into the bargain — By Jove! I should think he would marry.

* Bergerin, Marteau, Tiburce, Tuffler, Louis, Cæsar.

BERG. (*to* MART.) Shall we draw up the lease at once ? what do you say ?

TIB. (*to* MART.)　Shall we proceed ?

TUF.　It's a mere speculation.　He doesn't love the little darling.

CÆS. *and* LOU.　He never loved her.

TUF.　And should I suffer her to be thus sacrificed ?

LOU. *and* CÆS.　No !

TUF.　No !

MART. (*bewildered*).　There ! it begins again.　(*Goes up.*)

BERG. (*to* TUF.)　I say — you're not serious though, eh ?

TUF. (*crosses, and takes key from table*).　What's the reason I'm not serious ?　I'm so serious that I do not accept the candidate : my moral sense forbids.

MART.*　Well, but the key ?　Do you mean that you'll have the face —

TUF. (*puts it in his pocket*).　To keep it ?　I rather think so.

MART.　Yes ?　That is your final decision ?— you won't give it up of your own accord ?　Very well : then we'll force you to.

TUF.　We'll see about that.

MART.　Certainly ; for we shall have a majority. Quick, give me yours, Bergerin, so that we can have a majority.

BERG. (*pen and paper in hand*).　Yes, yes : I'll give it to you, — only suppose we sign the lease at once.

MART. (*exasperated*).　But, great Jupiter, man ! since you have my word, my word, my word —

CÆS.†　Since Tiburce has the pavilion.

---

* Bergerin, Tuffier (farther up), Cæsar (at back), Marteau, Tiburce, Louis.

† Cæsar, Bergerin, Marteau, Tiburce, Tuffier (farther up), Louis.

BERG. (*irresolute*). Yes.

TIB. Certainly.

CÆS. And the vegetable-garden.

BERG. Yes.

TIB. Of course.

CÆS. (*aside to* BERG.) The vegetable-garden, where their children will howl all day long.

BERG. (*draws back key*). Their children ?

CÆS. (*aloud*). For after all it's to be hoped there'll be a family.

TIB. (*smiling*). I should rather think there will.

BERG. (*frightened*). They mean to have children ?

MART. (*takes his head in his hands*). Here it comes again.

TUF.* And your windows that open on the garden —

CÆS. And on the pavilion —

TUF. They'll play all day —

CÆS. And squall all night.

TUF. It will be perfectly charming!

CÆS. All this rabble of brats.

LOU. Little Tiburces.

CÆS. Who will all smell of vanilla.

BERG. (*horrified*). No, no : I tell you no ! It would only need that to drive me mad. I tell you I won't have their children : let 'em go and breed somewhere else. I won't give up my key. (*Goes up.*)

TUF., LOU., *and* CÆS. Bravo, Bergerin !

CÆS. We've settled the majority.

MART. Oh ! I'm going mad ; my head splits ; I shall explode shortly, like a shell! † (*Sits* L., *in place of* BERGERIN.)

---

* Cæsar, Tuffier, Bergerin, Marteau, Tiburce, Louis.
† Cæsar, Marteau, Tuffier, Bergerin, Tiburce, Louis.

8

Tɪʙ. (*supplicating*). O Monsieur Bergerin!

Bᴇʀɢ. Will you just clear out, and carry your babies along.

Mᴀʀᴛ. (*rising*). Ah! that's the tone to be taken, is it? Well, then, no; he sha'n't go, and he shall marry in spite of all the devils, in spite of you, and in spite of this villain who has brought it all about. He shall marry in spite of the men, in spite of the women, and in spite of himself. Sit down there! (*Takes* Tɪʙᴜʀᴄᴇ *by collar, and forces him down in chair.*)

Tɪʙ. (*exhausted, aside*). I begin to have had about enough of getting married.

Mᴀʀᴛ. (*takes table and puts it in centre, knocking aside the other furniture*). And now for the notary, — quick! Placide, Placide, bring on your notary.

Nᴏᴛᴀʀʏ (*appears*). I think you called me.

Mᴀʀᴛ. Yes. (*Drags him to table.*) Sit there. (*To the others.*) I shall do without you and your keys. (*Forces* Nᴏᴛᴀʀʏ *to sit.*)

Bᴇʀɢ. *and* Tᴜꜰ.* How will you?

Mᴀʀᴛ. You are about to see. (*Grasps convulsively the* Nᴏᴛᴀʀʏ's *papers.*) Now write there, Notary, in continuation, " brings as dowry a pavilion, a vegetable-garden."

Nᴏᴛ. (*writing*). A vegetable-garden —

Mᴀʀᴛ. (*dictating*). And, moreover, an iron chest with a cover like that of a money-box; as to the contents of which, being invited to specify — (*To the others.*) I've been lawyer's clerk in my time. (Nᴏᴛᴀʀʏ *rises to congratulate;* Mᴀʀᴛᴇᴀᴜ *forces him to sit, and resumes dictation faster than ever.*) Invited to specify,

---

* Cæsar and Louis (near piano), Tiburce (seated), Marteau (standing), the Notary (seated), Bergerin (on causeuse), Tuffier (seated at extreme right).

the said Marteau declares it to be needless, and that he transfers to the intended bride the full title to said chest, with all that it may contain, whether in specie, bills, promissory notes, mortgages on real estate, jewels, and all other property of whatever name and nature. (*The No-*TARY, *alarmed at the rapidity of dictation, reaches out for ink.* MARTEAU *catches his hand, and puts it back on the paper, continuing with redoubled speed.*) The chest aforesaid, being hermetically closed by three locks to be delivered in this condition to the betrothed pair, and after the celebration of the marriage to be by them opened —

TUF. *and* BERG. Opened?

BERG. How?

MART. (*with majesty*). In whatever manner they may see fit.

BERG. That is, broken open.

MART. Broken! By them, if they please: I wash my hands of it. I have the chest, and I give it *(to the* NOTARY): is not that correct?

TUF. But you've no right to. (*Rises, takes his chair, and plants himself at table, back to audience.*) But, sir, he has no right to.

NOT. (*to* MART.)* Indeed.

MART. Well, I'll take the right.

NOT. (*to* TUF.) Ah! if he takes it — (*During the whole of this scene, the* NOTARY, *who occasionally disappears in the excited group of the three men, is occupied in avoiding accidents from their violent action.*)

BERG. (*to* NOT.) He undertakes to make over by deed what belongs to us.

NOT. (*to* MART.) Ah! that's not legal.

* Tiburce (seated), Notary (beyond table), Tuffier (seated before table), Bergerin (standing at right), Cæsar and Louis (standing at fireplace).

MART. I make over by deed what belongs to me.

NOT. That's another case.

TUF. It belongs to us three.

BERG. To us three.   .

NOT. (*to* MART.) Joint property, then: they are right.

MART. It belongs to me, to me! Here it is in my house, and bought eighteen years ago with my dollars; and I can show the receipt.

NOT. (*pulled about on all sides, to the others*). Individual property, then: he's in the right.

TUF. (*growing warm*). Bought on joint account.

BERG. On joint account.

NOT. (*to* MART.) Partnership property, then: you're in the wrong.

TUF. *and* BERG. (*triumphing*). Of course. (TUFFIER *crosses*, R.)

MART. (*takes* TUF's *chair, and plants himself to the left of* NOT.) But he don't understand any thing about it. There's been no contract of partnership.

NOT. (*to the others*). There's been no act of partnership. Then, what do you claim?

TUF. (*springs towards him angrily*). What's that? what do we claim?

NOT. (*frightened*). Excuse me.

TUF. (*furious*). There's no need of an act of partnership?

NOT. (*frightened*). Certainly —

BERG. A verbal agreement before witnesses is sufficient. (*Strikes on table, and passes*, L.)

NOT. Of course.

MART. (*strikes on table*). And I tell you it's insufficient.

NOT. Sometimes.

MART. (*shouts*). Always!

Not. (*trembling*). Always!

Tuf. (*threatening*). Never!

Not. Never.

Berg. (*rejoicing, and striking on table*). It's a partnership then, it's a firm. (*Crosses*, R.)

Not. That's true.

Mart. I deny it.

Not. (*losing his head*). You do right.

Berg. *and* Tuf. (*upon the* Not.) We maintain our assertion.

Not. (*shouts*). You are right!

Berg. Who's right?

Not. Oh the devil! (*Succeeds in getting loose, all rumpled and torn.*)

Mart. (*rising*). The course is perfectly simple : we will go to law about it.

Tuf. (*frightened*). Eh! *

Tib. A lawsuit now, for variety.

Cæs. (*aside*). All goes on famously.

Mart. And, if I should spend my last dollar in it, I'll drag you from court to court. I'll have the very ablest lawyer, — one that can muddle things up, and make it last three years.

Tuf. Three years!

Mart. And, during all that time, we shall never leave the Court House : we shall breakfast, dine, and sleep there.

Tuf. And my life will bothered out of me!

Mart. And your life will be bothered out of you.

Tuf. And I shall dream of black gowns and square caps! No, no : go to the devil! (*throwing down key*),

---

* Tiburce, seated; Notary, at back; Marteau, Tuffler, Bergerin, Louis, and Cæsar, at back.

8*

and fight it out between you. I'll have no more to do
with it.

Berg. (*sitting in centre; gayly*). I don't give in, —
devil a bit of it. A lawsuit will be quite an interesting
distraction for me.

Mart.* Oh, yes! But it will be in all the papers.
They'll publish our private life down to the smallest
details: so, for instance, everybody will known that Monsieur Bergerin is an old bachelor who has collected
thirty-six watches and eighty snuff-boxes.

Berg. (*gayly*). All right!

Mart.† And one of these days there will appear in
the police-reports: "A fearful crime has just spread con-
sternation through Batignolles" —

Berg. Eh!

Mart. (*continuing*). "Incited by cupidity, malefactors
introduced themselves, last night, into the sumptuous
suite of apartments inhabited alone by the rich Monsieur
Bergerin" —

Berg. (*frightened*). Into my rooms!

Mart. (*continuing*). And this morning, Madame
Placide, arriving to give her accustomed care to the
establishment, discovered the unfortunate proprietor
hanged to his bedpost.

Berg. (*horrified*). Hanged!

Mart. Hanged!

Tuf. Hanged!

Tib. Hanged!

Berg. (*screams*). Will you hold your tongues, and not
repeat such horrors! Ah! I'm all in a cold sweat.
Hanged! Here you may just go to the devil, the whole

---

* Tiburce, Notary, at back; Marteau, Bergerin, Cæsar, Louis, Tuffler.

† Notary, at back; Tiburce, Bergerin, Marteau, Cæsar, Louis, at back; Tuffier.

lot of you, — dowry, money-box, sons-in-law, and the whole shop. Hanged to the bedpost! Just take your old key, and rid me of it; only don't talk to me any more about any thing, — lawsuit, thieves, or marriage ; for I feel I'm just going crazy (*throws down key*), — just going crazy. (*Goes after the Notary.*)

Tib. (*who for some time has had movements indicating a nervous crisis*). (*Aside.*) So am I, so am I!

Mart. (*triumphing*). At last.

Lou. (*to Cæs.*) What shall we do?

Mart. (*brandishing keys*). Victory! The victory is ours. Come, son-in-law.

Tib. (*with nervous movements which he cannot repress*). (*Rising.*)* Your son-in-law. Excuse me, Monsieur Marteau : you are very good, and I respect you infinitely.

Mart. What is he making up faces at now?

Tib. Certainly: I should be immensely flattered — but there — frankly —

Mart. Well!

Tib. Well — (*The attack increases.*) No : you see, I never could get used to leading such an existence of the devil in a holy-water pot.

Lou. (*aside*). What's that he says?

Mart. What's that, — stuff?

Tib. (*with convulsive motions, and screaming*). Yes, I've had enough. I've had enough; and, rather than be your son-in-law, I'd choose to be condemned to the hand-organ for life.

Mart. Fire and fury! He refuses my daughter. (*Springing at Tiburce.*)

All (*holding him*). Monsieur Marteau!

Cæs. Uncle!

* Bergerin and Notary, at back; Cæsar, Tiburce, Marteau, Louis, Tuffier·

MART. Let me assassinate him!

TIB. (*grinding his teeth, and yelling*). Don't come near me! (*Noise, general row.*)

Enter MARION, LUCIE, PLACIDE, *very much scared.*

LUC. *and* MAR. What a noise!

PLAC. What's going on?

MART. (*bellowing*). Oh!

LUC. (*runs to* MART.) Papa!

MAR. (*runs to* MART.) What is it?

MART. (*pointing at* TIB.) It's he: it's that black-guard, that refuses to marry you.

MAR. (*joyfully*). He refuses then, — he?

MART. Yes, he!

Enter MADAME TUFFIER.

MAD. TUF. Louis refuses? That's false.

MART.* What?

TUF. (*to his wife*). Mind your own business!

MAD. TUF. My son has told me all. He has been sacrificed; but he never refused to marry.

MART. Who's talking about him?

MAD. TUF. Who is it you are at then?

MART. At him, — him. (*Points at* TIBURCE.)

MAD. TUF. Oh! go ahead then. (*Crosses to* R. *of* MARTEAU.)

MART. (*whose rage has turned to tears, taking* MAR. *in his arms*). Ah! my poor darling!

MAD. TUF. (*running on*). And so says I to myself, my son has faults, like other people; but he's incapable of treachery.

* Tiburce, Cæsar, Marion, Madame Tuffier, Marteau, Tuffier, Lucie, Notary, Bergerin.

MART. Great Jove! will you allow me to finish my sentence?

MAD. TUF. What! deny a mother the right to defend her offspring! (*Takes* LOUIS *in her arms.*)

MART. Tuffier, tie up your wife.

MAD. TUF. Lay hands upon me!

LOU. Mamma!

MAD. TUF. (*holding on to the* NOT.) Let them come: I am under the ægis of the law.

NOT. (*trying to get away*). Madame, you squeeze me too tight. (MADAME TUFFIER *begins to converse with him aside with great animation.*)

MART. (*who hardly knows where he is*). What was it I was just going to do?

LUC. (*pointing at* MAR.) Papa, you were just going to embrace her.

MART. (*affected*). Ah! so I was. Come, my child, — come to my arms. (CÆSAR *slips under* MARTEAU's *arm, and is kissed in the place of* MARION.) Who am I kissing here?

CÆS. O uncle! that kiss did me so much good! — don't take it away from me.

MART. (*sentimentally*). The poor boy is in the right after all. But for him, Marion would have been at this moment the wife of this booby.

CÆS. Whereas now she can be the wife of the little Louis, whom she loves as I love Lucie.

MART. Right, that's true: so she can. (*To* TIBURCE.) That shall be your punishment, you little wretch! (*To* LOUIS.) Marion is yours.*

LOU. Oh, rapture!

---

* Tiburce, Marion. Louis, Tuffier, Placide, Bergerin, Lucie. Cæsar, Notary (on causeuse), and Madame Tuffier (opposite).

MART. Placide, bring the money-box.

ALL Ah!

TUF. (*aside*). Yes, now we shall see.

MART. (*to* LOU.) Yes, I give you Marion. (PLACIDE *puts box on table.*) I give her to you with the whole contents of the money-box, — yes, all. (*Opens box.*)

BERG. (*looks in*). Nothing!

TUF. Nothing?

LUC., CÆS., PLAC., MAR. Nothing whatever.

TIB. (*aside, rubs his hands*). Nothing whatever. Well, I am in luck.

MART. (*to* TUF. *and* BERG.) Oh, this is disgusting!

TUF. Well, after all —

BERG. You didn't put any thing in either.

MART. I, — I was bringing up Marion.

TUF. I was bringing up my son.

BERG. And I —

CÆS. You were bringing up rabbits.

TIB. (*laughing, aside*). Well, I'm glad now I didn't go.

MART. (*looking at* TIB., *who laughs*). He laughs. The villain triumphs.

MAD. TUF. (*to the* NOT.) What stuff is that you tell me? — that the wife must follow everywhere?

NOT. (*who feels ill*). I assure you, madame, I am in want of air.

(MADAME TUFFIER *continues to hold him back.*)

MAD. TUF. You are an idiot.

TUF. (*to* CÆS. *and* LOU., *who are talking to him*). Without dowry — oh, get out! Forty thousand francs, or no marriage.

MART.* I've got my revenge now. (*Gesticulates under* TIBURCE's *nose.*) I'll give the forty thousand francs.

TIB. (*ceases laughing*). Ah, bah!

CÆS. O uncle!

MAR. My good papa !

MART. (*nervously*). Yes, I'll give them. (*Takes notes from pocket-book, and brandishes them under* TIBURCE's *nose.*) I dower Marion, and I dower her alone (*measuring* TUFFIER *and* BERGERIN); and I forbid any one else to put a red cent in the box (*angrily*), — I forbid them.

BERG. You forbid them? — you forbid them?

MART. Yes, I forbid them.

BERG. If we desired to —

MART. I defy you.

BERG. You defy us?

MART. Yes.

BERG. (*takes out pocket-book*). You defy me, do you? (*Puts it up again.*) Well, you are perfectly right.

MART. (*turns towards* TIB.) Well, miscreant, you refused my daughter, did you? You prefer the hand-organ, eh? Well, Marion has found a husband and forty thousand francs of dowry.

TIB. (*aside*). Forty thousand francs! The devil! Now I'm sorry I staid.

MART. Now for the notary : quick.

CÆS. Quick, now for the notary.

NOT. (*in centre, bewildered*). This riot, screaming, and tumult! — ah, ah, ah! I don't know what's got me.

---

* Tiburce, Lucie, and Marion (farther up), Placide (at back), Cæsar, Louis (at back), Marteau, Bergerin, Tuffier, Notary (at window), Madame Tuffier (on causeuse).

Cæs. (*looks at* Not., *who is convulsed*). Well, what has got him?

Not. I think I'm going to have a nervous crisis.

Cæs. He too? Down to the notary. (*All crowd round him.*)

Marion, Louis, Marteau, Tiburce (behind, on chair), Placide, Notary, Tuffier
Lucie, Bergerin, Madame Tuffier (on sofa), Cæsar.

CURTAIN.